French
POSTCARDS

Jane Merchant

Spinsters Ink
2006

This novel is a work of fiction. Names, characters, places and incidents either are the product of the author's imagination or are used fictitiously. Any resemblance to actual persons, living or dead, events, or locales is entirely coincidental.

Copyright© 2006 by Jane Merchant

Spinsters Ink, Inc.
P.O. Box 242
Midway FL 32343

Printed in the United States of America on acid-free paper
First Edition

Editor: Anna Chinappi
Cover designer: LA Callaghan

ISBN 1-883523-67-2

for Brigitte

Visit

Spinsters Ink

at

spinstersink.com

or call our toll-free number

1-800-301-6860

Acknowledgments

Special thanks first to Linda Hill who plucked this book out of obscurity and brought it to life. To my editor Anna Chinappi who taught me everything I never learned in college. To my friends Barbara Williams, Sylvie Delaby and Carmen Radulescu for loving this book, not just to be nice, but because they thought it was good. To Rebecca Ramsey and Susan Wallace who encouraged me from the earliest stages when this book began. And especially to my mother for never freaking out and my sister for her steadfast belief and encouragement. And, surtout, to Robert for putting up with it all and letting me write. *Et merci a la belle France!*

2004
French Postcards

*Beware of swoons, . . . A frenzy fit is not one quarter so pernicious;
it is an exercise to the Body and if not too violent, is I dare say
conductive to Health in its consequences—Run mad as often as
you chuse; but do not faint.*

—Mansfield Park

Part I

Pardon my French

1

Mrs. Randall, a short, stout woman of forty, stood in her aquamarine nylon running suit and sneakers, her wide brown eyes peering up at Elinor with intensity.

"Ever since I saw little Toby Kimbal run out into traffic here, I have been asking Madame Lambert to have somebody stand here at the gate. I am terrified some little one will try to escape out into the street."

Mrs. Randall, the detector of all wickedness and injustice in the world, could discover bad intentions in the most benign situations as well as she could the perfect piece for her entryway. Teachers were always ruining her children's minds while ignoring their obvious talents. She could spot Lupus in the achiness of a cold and pneumonia in a cough. Her children were regularly quarantined for bronchitis, otitis and gastroenteritis. In her view, the school was not unlike a jungle in its savageness and the threats it posed her Jeremy, an uncommonly sensitive child, and little Taylor. She sent them out to play armored in helmets, insect repellent and sunscreen and always called them home regularly to replenish their fluids. And although she insisted she was by no means the authority on parenting, or housekeeping, and her children were certainly not perfectly turned out, other people's children were sadly neglected and their homes vulgar. From the very beginning and without the slightest encouragement, she had sought Elinor's confidence in many of her domestic concerns—PMS, irregular pap smears, and the nutritional completeness of peanut butter. Elinor always listened with a kind of amazement for her candor, nodding and agreeing that she should undoubtedly take Richard to a specialist for his relentless snoring. Yes, she would agree, it was highly probable that he had sleep apnea, and people could die of that you know. Not to mention, why did he fall asleep so suddenly and under the most bizarre of circumstances if he didn't have some sort of condition?

It was a gray, rather gloomy day in October, and these women from the South shivered in their light Windbreakers against the unpleasant climate of this godforsaken land. They were in a constant state of denial that the weather could be like this in October.

Mrs. Randall lowered her voice in conspiracy, "If some little child were to get hurt, I just want to be sure I have done *everything* in my power to prevent it."

Elinor had heard this persistent concern of hers several times before. The school was entirely understaffed, harsh, and continually neglecting the enormous responsibility of looking after the children properly.

"I volunteered myself to do it," Mrs. Randall continued sacrificially, "and they refused, saying something about how it would violate school regulations to have an unemployed person responsible for that, or something." She didn't really know what the whole cold French rejection of her charitable and earnest concern was all about. It seemed perfectly irrational and unjust. "I am always aware of it anyway," she said with wounded dignity.

"I know Harriet, it's very good of you," Elinor offered her in comfort. And Mrs. Randall looked pleased enough with her approval, which is perhaps all she wanted—approval for her concern and effort to gain some control over a mysterious world that seemed to be pulling away from the curb like a bus she was running after, leaving her in a haze of choking exhaust. Elinor remembered her own difficulty leaving Alexi at the *maternelle* for the first time two years ago behind the bleak battlements of the old building, handing her little girl over to the maiden school teacher with the face of an angel, sweet but cold, like the painted face of a statue of a saint in a church. Elinor watched the woman take Alexi's little hand in what she was sure was her icy, smooth porcelain one and lead her into the classroom. Detachment and resignation was required to leave the child there and turn away alone, to wonder what would happen to her during the day, while she busied herself at home with the routine of her domestic chores that were essentially the same in France as they would be in the States and for that they were comforting.

Alexi did not cry that day. She was too much bewildered and thoroughly curious. She spent the whole year, hopelessly loving the beautiful statue that was her teacher, who calmly cooed her flock of three-year-olds to order and discipline, who gently wiped and pulled up the troops' underpants after they had all been marched to the communal potty, a row of miniature white porcelain flushable toilettes. Elinor wished many times that the teacher could love Alexi as much as she wanted her to, wished, or believed that she did, or at least fake it in the way the warm and cuddly kindergarten teachers did in the States. But the teacher remained always just out of reach, smiling her serene smile down on her little charges and putting together a marvelous and flawlessly choreographed end-of-the-year pageant where she had amazingly organized a group of over twenty pre-schoolers into making their own costumes and dancing in a sea of blue and green streamers, fish in the sea, to the voice of Harry Bellefonte.

Elinor passed the faces of the other French mothers in the corridor never feeling anything but polite tolerance toward these elegant and delicate creatures who brought their children each day to Mademoiselle Valmont's class. They reminded her of sixties housewives, resigned to their feminine duties of child bearing and rearing in haughty solitude, dressed in decidedly unpretentious chic. They didn't band together as the American women did, sharing the intimate details of their domestic lives with frank wisecracks and cheerful candor. They were so maddeningly reserved, formal and elegant, tittering to each other with an insupportable femininity that was enormously self-conscious, superficial and, Elinor was sure, never interesting. *Surely they must discuss these things as we do*, she thought and was determined to improve her French in an effort to discover what it was they *did* talk of. But even after two years she had never gotten involved in a conversation with a French woman that was ever any deeper or more revealing than an intricate discussion of the mating habits and behavior of bees and the delicious varieties of unpasteurized honey they produced, *par exemple*, or mushrooms—a favorite topic in Auvergne. Had she taken advantage of the numerous varieties of mushrooms in the region? The Frenchwomen might tell of a *morille* that they found in the garden the other day, or where one could go to collect truffles in the forest.

But that day, at the beginning of Alexi's third school year, Elinor looked past Harriet Randall's head, momentarily distracted by something extraordinary. A tall, dark-haired woman, bent down and effortlessly lifted her small daughter up onto her shoulders and carried her past them, out of the courtyard and onto the street. The woman led with her free hand another tiny boy and her two older, beautiful daughters followed behind. At once, everything about the woman was vigorous, strong and fine, nothing like Elinor had ever seen before. There is never anything so startling as a beautiful woman rendered more obvious among a great many dull and tedious members in the crowd of the school yard that day, and Elinor tried not to gape. She tried to pretend to Harriet she was listening to her, reluctantly taking her gaze from the woman and settling it on Harriet's very ordinary features. She said something, "you're absolutely right, they should do something," and turned back to look in feigned concern for any other wayward child, past the gate after the woman, walking it seemed in slow motion, her long strides, carrying her up the sidewalk, her mane of dark hair loose to her shoulders. Elinor would not admit then that she had chosen her as decidedly as if she had stated out loud to Mrs. Randall, "she's the one."

She turned back and looked at Mrs. Randall. Mrs. Randall appeared to be talking, telling her something, and Elinor fixed her gaze on her animated face and watched her lips moving, but she didn't hear what she was saying. It was as if a tea kettle were singing in her ears that she was only slightly conscious of, gently nudging her from a slumber of routine and drudgery which threatened to consume her youth, beauty and wit.

For a long time Elinor had forgotten about herself and instead delighted in everything about her children. She was astonished at just how perfect and beautiful they were when they were born. First, she thought of them just as babies—something for her to admire and love. She showed them off with pride, paying special attention to what they wore—that she wiped their mouths with a soft cotton Baby Dior washcloth and had all the proper accessories to care for them. Then she grew tired of fussing over them and didn't quite know what to do with them. They began to become themselves, not a part of her, which was not always pleasing. And she began to realize how ill-suited she might be in shaping and encouraging their little emerging personalities. Babies had rather straightforward needs—to be changed, fed and bathed. It was like caring for plants, or pets. Children, however, were complex, difficult creatures that she feared could drain every drop of life from her with insatiable appetites for love and attention. She was entirely inadequate, although she was aware of the consequences. She could nurture them into accomplished young women or see them emerge as sullen teenagers with dubious pursuits, victims of the worst thing—low self-esteem! She shuddered to think of them attaching themselves to disreputable youths on skateboards in sagging jeans that threatened to expose their buttcrack. It was terrifying really.

Looking for Alexi's bright head among the other children let out from school and seeing her skip and play, like a stranger's child in a park or crowd, she was filled with wonder. Watching them for long moments while they slept, listening to their steady, soft snores, and admiring their wet pink mouths open—their little fists with the thumbs sticking out, laying nearby, having just fallen out in that delightful moment of perfect sleep, she was slightly envious. She admired their plump thighs and tiny feet, the softness of their flawless tender skin and nibbled their ears and fingers, biting their little bellies, smelling their baby smell and hearing the music of their baby laugh. She recognized that within their perfect little bodies lurked the fulfillment of all her hopes and dreams, or miserable failure and loss that could be devastating. Considering it now, the years had not passed quickly. Her absorption seemed to consume a lifetime of attention, even though Alexi was only six.

Until that moment, she could have spent her life arranging the perfect setting for her children like a picture in a magazine, framing photographs—professionally posed pictures taken in studios of her children in their best clothes, hair combed and tucked neatly into barrettes. She should cultivate a garden that grew strawberries and raspberry bushes, she thought. *They shall have an enormous house when I get home, with gardens to explore, just like in the* Secret Garden. *And there, they will grow into princesses, and I will go to church and pray and smile more and talk softly in a motherly tone that is always patient and comforting and God will hear my prayer,* she told herself.

It was not unlikely that many women like her, who shared a similar luxurious life as she did, with very little to do in the way of housework, children in school, dinner in the oven, or dinner that could be picked up somewhere, didn't have similar feelings of idleness, boredom or uselessness. Certainly in a world with so few vexations, discontent is likely to flourish.

Her life was not hard like the lives of the unfortunate people she watched from the vantage point of the television in her stylishly decorated living room—refugees escaping Afghanistan or some other unfortunate nation. She never feared her children might die of cholera or diphtheria as women did a hundred years ago, or in places far enough away from her that they might as well have vanished into the time when they had ever posed a threat to a woman like herself. Elinor had no worries except for perhaps that she wasn't gorgeous enough or that her children were just little beasts instead of pleasing little civilized creatures that everyone could praise. Americans expect unruly children. The French are horrified by them.

Perhaps she was silly and romantic because she believed in the spell that France had cast over her from the moment she landed in the world's most absurd airport—eerily like the French themselves, cold, daunting and thoroughly confusing, making you feel that if there was just a map, a guide, or if their intentions were more clearly labeled you could figure them out.

Everything one has ever heard or read about France is true—that it is a paradise of color, texture and history, and a gastronomic palace of delectable delicacies as varied as the landscape itself. And she lived in Auvergne, among the ancient volcanoes, sunflower and wheat fields of a Van Gogh painting, not Paris or the Sud-Est as all other expatriates or Francophiles choose for themselves. No, she didn't live in the most glamorous city in the world, which Paris undeniably is, or France's most beautiful region, the Sud-Est. She lived in the rather gloomy industrial city of Cherbourg which sometimes seemed to piss down sooty rain for at least six months out of the year. And even if it didn't, it gave that impression anyway.

Although the countryside was beautiful, the dreary city was built largely out of black volcanic stone. The magnificent black church distinguished the city as *la Ville Noire*—the city with the highest concentration of alcoholics and suicides throughout all of France. Even the French themselves complained of Auvergnats as unpleasant, grumpy people who kept themselves shut up behind their *volets* and prided themselves on being even more disagreeable than Parisians, who were by comparison, unseemingly tolerant of tourists and welcoming to newcomers.

In a way, she had sought the adventure of it since she had started at an early age devouring every type of fable and fairy tale that would take her out of her ordinary existence and transport her into someone else's life, one less bleak than her own. Her head was full of novels, ordinary life was always much too narrow for her. She was never a very good student, but always a great reader and at seventeen, when her French professor announced the possibility of going to France, Elinor was determined. Maybe something would happen to her, she hoped. She had never shown any extraordinary academic promise and was a miserable French student, but she had saved enough money, about a thousand dollars, from all of her part-time jobs and she told her mother she was going to spend it on the trip.

She visited Bretagne and Normandy in the cold drizzle of March. She packed all of her most romantic sweaters and boots, no sneakers or sweatshirts, and a stylish short trench coat that she wore with the collar turned up against the unpleasant climate. She drank *chocolat* for breakfast and wine with her tomato salad and steak *frites* at dinner. Everything was so exotic and foreign about France—the little tin Citroens all had yellow headlights at the time, the *Epoque d 'Or* interiors of the cafés, the freedom to drink beer with lunch in the afternoon and the secondhand vintage fashion she spent her money on in the open air flea markets in Montmartre. She stayed two weeks with a Parisienne girl her age in the girl's mother's apartment in Montparnasse. From her bedroom window, Elinor could see the tip of the Eiffel Tower, the most arresting sight in the world she had ever seen, she was convinced. And Caroline, the girl, wore a leather bomber before it was a cool thing to do in the States. The orange Renault 4 the girl's brother picked her up in from the train station had the stick shift stuck out from the dashboard and it could barely pull the three of them through the streets of Paris without a great deal of effort. And Elinor stood with Caroline and her girlfriends out on the street between her classes at the private all-girls Catholic school and smoked cigarettes—*Gitanes*—literally, *Gypsies*.

2

By evening Elinor had forgotten the whole strange incident, and urging herself to chop the vegetables for the ratatouille she would serve that night, she was easily convinced by the recommencement of the routine that what she had seen that afternoon was nothing extraordinary. After all, women could carry children on their shoulders, even French women. And she would no more allow herself to be thrilled by the sight of a strange woman on the playground than to run off on a whim to join the traveling *cirque* come to town.

She slapped Clara on the hand quickly for poking her fingers into the polenta she had just taken out of the oven, and the child looked up at her with indignation, snatching her hand away and comforting the wounded thing with her other hand against her body.

"I'm going to go and live with one of the French mommies!" Clara declared dramatically. Elinor stared at her in awe. She stamped her little foot in an absolutely charming display of disapproval for the ill-treatment of her precious little self. Elinor turned away, enamored of her beauty.

She dare not show her weakness for this child, who at four was already quite aware of her power and an expert at getting whatever she wanted. She would be fought over all of her life, Elinor suddenly knew. The image of the woman she had seen that morning sprang into her mind again, leading her pack home from school in a little parade. The woman seemed so magnificent, moving up the sidewalk with the natural grace of some beautiful animal and Elinor was suddenly sure it would indeed be preferable to be the daughter of such an elegant creature than to be the unfortunate child of such an inadequate mother. She dashed the image from her mind and moved about the kitchen, mechanically turning out a reasonably good dinner.

Elinor's husband came home that evening, and she felt she had never been so relieved to see him. Victor Dumitru, so steadfast and earnest, exceptionally good-natured and handsome, always tolerated her outrageous passions that she might fly into without notice or warning. Nothing was lacking in their relationship. She was never dissatisfied or taken for granted. He was an excellent father and marvelously intelligent in whatever it was he did as a respected engineer at Durtol. He brought home very impressive-looking reports filled with spectacular charts and graphs of analysis, and if he complained occasionally of being neglected, she would always say that he needed to bring home another one of his important-looking reports, as nothing could summon up her desire like an example of his brilliance, or watching him sign the monthly payment on her student loan which made her know he was always very valuable to her, sharing the burden of their family life with the patience and calm she lacked.

Victor was Romanian and they met in graduate school. He had immigrated to the States as a young man, and she had been captivated by his exotic foreignness and gypsy beauty. His wonderful unspoiled nature seemed always to celebrate his blessings and never take any of his good fortune for granted.

He was brilliant, educated in French at the top engineering university in Bucharest, so that when he was offered the job with Durtol, the French rubber and sporting goods manufacturer, it seemed to suit his background so naturally that when he asked her to marry him, she agreed. He seemed so sincere, and determined, she couldn't help but get caught up in it herself. She didn't want to disappoint all his good wishes or hurt his feelings, and it did seem easier than dumping him. Somehow they both understood that she was his reward for making it in the States and in the ugliest moments of their disputes, she reminded him of this. She was twenty-six. It seemed an appropriate next step. And after all the young men she had dated in the city, none were so sincere with so much determination, direction and conviction—all admirable qualities in a man. He was also one of the only men she had dated who didn't wing out their weenie at the end of a first date as if it were a token, or a compliment. It did seem a rare quality in this capricious day and age to be so certain of what one wanted, and she realized that her single criteria for marrying him was that he loved her. He was crazy in love she knew, and isn't that what a woman wants—to be adored, to validate her worth by having some handsome European stranger carry her off to Transylvania, or to France anyway? She thought of Jane Austen. "After all, happiness in marriage is entirely a matter of chance. If the dispositions of the parties are ever so well known to each other, or ever so similar beforehand, it does not advance their felicity in the least. They always continue to grow sufficiently unlike afterward to have their share of vexation, and it is better to know as little as possible of the defects of the person with whom you are to pass your life."

Their differences had caused conflict surely enough throughout their marriage, but for a woman, love is generally a rather selfish and exacting emotion. It gratifies the vanity of youth and secures and protects her in life and old age. Women who never marry are always out there in that chaos of dating whatever is left—pursuing unsavory relationships with dubious persons who are always very disappointing. Marriage has changed very little over time, and it is still what people do—a simple compromise, sex in exchange for comfort and security. Happily, their marriage had started out superficially, based on little more than attraction, but had grown into a strong attachment of implacable honesty that defied resentment. Which is the best possible way a marriage can evolve. Their attraction remained, strengthened by the glue of shared experiences and responsibilities, resilient to the usual vexations that occur between married people. Quite like brother and sister, she might have slugged her brother with all her might when they were children, but it had never altered their love or separated them in anyway.

Elinor was never bored with him. They were as well suited for each other as any two people could be. She was never searching for some lack of romance in their relationship, or trying to spice it up with kinky sex, or an affair, when comfort and convenience seemed always more satisfying. More often *she* was reluctant, as if she were being urged to accept another helping after a generous meal, as if sex were some kind of necessary examination required of her to stay healthy in a relationship before her next checkup, although she performed her duties as blithely as any mistress could. Sometimes sex was just another hurdle in the steeplechase after the kids had been bathed, teeth brushed, put into their pajamas, read to and put to bed. She was never disappointed in the fact that Victor had not torn her dress off in years as other heroines in novels are portrayed as becoming bored in their marriages to respectable men who remain faithful, making quiet love to them while keeping steady employment, instead of being a freelance photographer off shooting on location in India for *National Geographic*, or some cowboy capable of rendering horses as helpless to his skillful love-making as women, like a character in a Robert Waller novel or the movie version, the heroine surely to be played by Kristin Scott Thomas, waiting on her porch for Clint Eastwood to drive up in a pickup truck named Harry. Although Elinor should allow no one to play her in the movie version of herself *except* Kristin Scott Thomas.

It was Victor who brought her here, answered at the most inconvenient time, her longing for adventure that she felt she must have since that dream-like time when she was seventeen and had her first glimpse at what it was like to be carried away on a journey beyond her own borders. And then there she was, with Alexi just three wearing only a diaper and eight-month-old Clara. Both Alexi and Clara had gotten diarrhea, and from Atlanta to Paris and finally to Cherbourg, Elinor had run out of changes of clothes.

Tired and hungry, they reached their temporary apartment—a rather bleak, tunnel-like dwelling, furnished with sterile furnishings and a rotary telephone whose ring clanged and echoed, traveling through the corridor like a steel ball winding down a complex network of piping. Elinor was terrified of it, and she would answer the calls from her mother with the same urgency she might have snatched a child to safety from being hit by a bus.

After a two-hour nap with their chins bent to their chests, their heads against the long, cylindrical uni-pillow on the bed, which was a bit more like a hammock and complained noisily with any movement, they were refreshed enough to take in their first impressions of Cherbourg and hunt about for their dinner. The day was windy, a bit too windy Elinor couldn't help thinking, for August. What business did it have being so windy? The wind stirred and dislodged the dirt, filth and small particles from the deteriorating buildings, as moldy as old cheese.

There is nothing particularly charming about Cherbourg, except for perhaps the idea that it is not at all charming. One has to look hard to see the beauty. It is in the details, not in the whole. If Paris wears its heart on its sleeve then Cherbourg locks up its heart behind heavy dungeon doors. It is as miserable as Manchester, or Stoke-on-Trent. Even the wine, once grand, is inferior, the vines having suffered a devastating blight in the mid-nineteenth century. Its history is utilitarian, although the French have never seemed to have the taste for work, *sauf* the artisans, *viticulteurs* or cheese makers. Everything about the inevitable industrialization on the road to modernism the world has taken seems to defy the very heart of France. This is perhaps most evident in the absolute poetry of the countryside's storybook castles, so fanciful, in contrast to the ugliness of the modern buildings in the city. They have no talent for it. Offices are unpleasant, cheap and uninspired, constructed of cement blocks stacked on top of one another. The frustrations the American has in living in France is its absolute refusal to be efficient and keep up. Its entire lack of interest in the rat race seems so exasperating.

Elinor followed Victor and the children past tattoo parlors with greenish Polaroids on the windows of the decorated skin of strange body parts and crevices, not at first evident. Is that an armpit, she wondered? There were sad little shops that sold odd bits of merchandise that had no apparent relationship to each other—Chinese dolls, a pair of sunglasses, lingerie and a selection of Harley-Davidson cigarette lighters. They finally came across the famous *crêperie Le1513*, but since none of them were much in the mood for crêpes, they each ordered dubious *menus* of tough, tasteless meat and soggy *frites*—not a very good representation of the fabulous French cuisine Elinor had prepared herself for or she remembered from when she was a young girl. Elinor wondered if perhaps she was finished with her curiosity to explore new places, wandering the streets for a bit of culture, a hidden bookstore, or pleasant café. Instead, she wondered what she would do with her children here, dodging pigeon poop and dog shit, watching Alexi playing and swinging on a heavy chain fence, pressing her face, wide-eyed against a shop window to look at rows of the chipped porcelain heads of antique dolls. Although she sensed from the very beginning, that next morning, waking up in the cold apartments of their temporary dwelling, despite the fact that this time nothing directly spoke to her, that this was fun, or exotic, there was something indeed delicious in the breakfast and coffee she prepared. Even the eggs were more delicious, with bright orange yolks. The *confiture* and pastries they fed upon suggested the promise of something wonderful here in France for them to taste.

They dealt with the bleakness of the temporary apartment by dining on the marvelous food she found in the marketplace, while they searched the city for a house. On Saturday, the *marché* Saint Pierre was made nearly impassable by the crowds picking over the berries, nuts, mushrooms, figs, *charcuterie*, cheese, wine, live fowl and small game. The spit roasted chicken tasted as if it had been fed on milk and grain and they soaked up the juice with delicious *pain de campagne* baked in stone ovens. She once asked a notable chef in Cherbourg what he thought was the most delicious French dish. A good *poulet roti*, he said without hesitation.

Elinor carried on the routine of bringing and taking the children to school with a startling new awareness of the beautiful woman in the courtyard of the school. Victor woke her at seven. He had been up since dawn. He had showered, shaved, turned on the gas to take the chill off the house for her and the children and was busily making the breakfast and coffee. He never seemed tired as she was of the routine, rather he thrived on it, was entirely content and satisfied in her and the children.

Elinor got out of bed with some purpose and went into the bathroom. She looked in the mirror and saw herself as other people might see her—men, her husband, the woman on the playground—already the romantic image of her began to fill Elinor's mind. She washed her face. She liked her appearance. Although she might not be beautiful, she had certain qualities that might convince people that she was. She was tall and handsome, the remarkable quality few women possessed of seasoning and growing better with age. She seemed to emerge from herself, the extra flesh of her youth and of motherhood was carved away each year to reveal more of herself, strong, lean and fit. Victor remarked on it, and it gave her some feeling of singularity, separated her somehow from her average existence among other women who shared her situation, and made her an actress in her role—a movie star even.

She dressed herself. Then she roused the children and dressed them in a menagerie of bright layers of patterned sweaters and tights. The children would be at school all day, let out twice to run and play on the courtyard whether it sleeted or rained.

"There she is," Victor said to the girls proudly, when she came down to breakfast. "Look at your mommy." He was always proud of her. He was still old-fashioned in this modern world he had adopted. She was every bit his and he took good care of her as a valued possession. She was embarrassed to admit that she treasured herself as such and made sure she met his expectations.

She laughed. "What?"

"You look pretty, that's all."

She felt suddenly silly as if there was no reason at all that she should, given the day that awaited her.

"I'm shopping in Venice today with the ladies, I'm sure," she said to poke fun at her leisurely lifestyle. They did this all the time, she acting bored and pampered over the coffee that he had made.

"I might even go to the cinema with Karen this afternoon." She had nothing but time to fill, before she picked the girls up at four o'clock, since she didn't work while they were in France. He raised an eyebrow.

"Are you taking Alexi to the pool after school?"

"Yes," she said dully.

"Do not imagine I should be grateful for this life you have confined me to," she remembered shouting dramatically at him once. I shall go mad, she thought, staring at the fish they kept in captivity on the kitchen counter, dreading the thought of coming back to the empty house after seeing her children off to school. She looked at Victor in his neat shirt and tie, gently urging Clara with a spoonful of yogurt—he was impossibly patient and good.

"Did you feed Gumdrop?" Elinor asked Alexi in an overly cheery voice that sounded sickening to her. She stood at the counter, watching the fish swim wildly around the bowl, drinking her coffee lethargically, waiting for it to jar her to action. *I will not go mad, oh no, I will not! I will not go mad, said the fish in the pot!* What am I doing here? she asked herself, but said instead, "He must be hungry," although she feared it was neurotic.

"I get to feed him today!" Clara said excitedly, and Alexi hesitated, considering if she should allow this or not and then good-naturedly nodded her approval in an off-handed manner. Elinor was astonished. Such good children, healthy and beautiful. Clara got down from her chair and ran around the kitchen counter. Clara would do anything not to eat her breakfast.

"No, not until you finish your cereal," Elinor said. "Don't forget your suit Alexi, you have swimming today."

Alexi nodded her brown head, munching a mouthful of cereal. The girls had to be at school by eight-thirty. Elinor put them in the car, kissed Victor good-bye and drove them to town. Today, she thought, she was eager to drop the children, hand them over as it were to someone else for a while, but as soon as she did she would miss them terribly and be lonely.

Bringing Clara to her class, Elinor inevitably ran into the beautiful dark-haired Frenchwoman, who she discovered had her little boy and girl in Clara's class. Elinor and the woman exchanged looks, noticing each other with an assumed familiarity, although they never spoke a word. She had seen the woman's little girl approach Clara, say her name and take her hand to play. Plump, sturdy and fair, the little girl had her mommy's face and air. The boy, apparently the little girl's twin, was also in the same class. He had his mother's beautiful dark hair but without his sister's sense of confidence. He was more unsure, following his sister around, clearly entirely taken with her sense of the world, herself. This quality in the little girl fascinated Clara enough for her to follow her into the classroom agreeably, forgetting about her mother entirely.

After dropping the children off, the American women arranged themselves in front of the gate in impenetrable bastions of English, being generally boisterous and guffawing about a particular mishap, misstep, faux pas or some recent flea market find. Elinor would join them briefly to chat before going off to do the shopping, the cleaning and her other domestic duties. On Tuesday and Thursday mornings she went to the supermarket, and in the afternoons she ardently studied French at the university. She was making excellent progress and she enjoyed it immensely. It was her passion and extraordinary love of language that allowed her to succeed. The delightful expressions and turns of phrase in French charmed her so that she listened intently and tried to memorize everything her instructor said in case she might get the chance to speak to the Frenchwoman. On Wednesday and Friday mornings she worked out at the gym. Wednesday she picked up the girls for lunch and took Alexi to gymnastics in the afternoon. That left Mondays to visit the hairdresser, take Victor's shirts to the cleaners, vacuum, or simply stay at home and sit and stare at the yellow wallpaper. She contented herself in the banal routine of it.

Her duty lay in scheduling her children with play dates, pick-ups for lunch, or activities that she convinced herself trained them in everything they needed for life. Most of the American women rescued their children for lunch at noon instead of leaving them to eat with the other French children, thus sparing them, if only for an hour or so the natural humiliations that lurked in the lunchroom or on the playground afterward.

Elinor had lived in France for two years already among a rather daunting clique of other expatriate women, mothers like herself with little to do but wonder what shoes to wear to the school gate in the afternoon to receive their precious children from the severe custody they had to endure at the private Catholic school of Cherbourg. Everyone knew each other with an immediate intimacy that characterized being an American expatriate in France. The shared situation of being *etrangers* in France and speaking the same language made them cling to each other in league against the French while demonstrating a certain level of Francophilia at the same time. It was important to be as French as possible, cultivate French friends and practice French cuisine or at least a gastronomic appreciation for it. There was a certain competitive atmosphere present in this which made the women rank themselves according to experience and expertise, admiring or despising in turn each other's French accents, savoir faire or alma maters, comfort in child-rearing, hair, purse, scarf or a great favorite—to compare with a rather nasty competitiveness, their children. Because any kind of natural competition between females that you sensed was rather catty as an adolescent, or among your girlfriends in college, becomes deliberately bitter and malicious among women with children, whose own beauty and talents become increasingly less apparent or important. They really had little to do but enjoy Europe as their playground and have the French educate their children for a time, something that might become intolerable in the long term as Elinor was made daily aware by the relentless comparisons and complaints that demonstrated all the inferior points of the brutal French practices.

There seemed to be some unspoken desperation that lurked behind the otherwise pleasant faces of these women whose lives had been thrown out of orbit when they had been asked to uproot from their quiet lives of playgroup and swimming lessons at the subdivision pool back home and follow their husbands, *good God*, to France, where nothing was like anything they were used to.

Deborah Knolls, quick, capable and well-bred, stopped and waited for Elinor as she helped Alexi and Clara out of the car to walk them up to the school. Deborah was a pert redhead, pretty and pregnant, who had undoubtedly been a cheerleader in high school and was perhaps still capable of doing a cartwheel or maybe even the splits.

"Bonjour Alexi and Clara," Deborah said deliberately loud, Elinor couldn't help noticing, to encourage her two girls to do the same. They both repeated a dutiful 'bonjour' in a blasé duet.

"I know, my mother always said, 'no white shoes after September,' but she insisted on these shoes this morning, so I gave in," Deborah said, assuming Elinor had paid any attention at all to the shoes.

"This morning, if someone would have offered me fifty bucks, I would have given them Molly," Deborah declared.

She was bound to convivial wisecracks or talk of dry cleaning, investments and celebrity gossip. Her pretty little girls stood before Elinor's girls like mommy accessories, dressed immaculately in preppy pinafores. Little Molly had on white tights and white patent leather shoes as if she had no intention of playing at all. Deborah stood by Elinor's car, waiting for her so that they could walk to the school gate together. Elinor leaned in over the backseat to retrieve the girls *cartables*—the square school bags they wore strapped to their backs.

"Oh, I know, Elinor," Deborah said, peering into her car, "I decided to lower my standards too, and let the baguette crumbs fall where they may. I can't seem to keep my car clean either. Here in France, it's impossible to keep your car clean unless you vacuumed every day."

Elinor raised her hand above her eyes briefly to cut the glare and survey the back seats covered with crumbs, miscellaneous bits of paper, toys, etc. She was surprised Deborah had any interest in stopping to talk. There was very little chance they could have anything to say to one another given any topic of conversation, and Elinor was sure that what she was wearing inspired little interest and less admiration. She couldn't help wondering if Deborah had seen her socks over the top of her boots while her jeans were high enough to reveal them as she got out of the car. They were Victor's socks, grayish from the wash with two black stripes at the top and one, she knew, was inside out. Of course Deborah had noticed with a kind of secret joy. Elinor was sure Deborah didn't miss the fact that she had been wearing the same sweater and jeans for days either, had some clairvoyant knowledge that only moments before arriving at school, she had frantically searched the car for something, a coat, a jacket, umbrella, didn't she have something else to wear? Her purse, at last she hit on. Maybe she could wear her purse, she thought.

Deborah Knolls had lived in France nearly as long as Elinor, but had never allowed herself to be dismayed, frightened or discouraged by the

French simply by never feeling any need to struggle with their language. Deborah refused to think that any effort to do so might reduce her feelings of frustration and dependence on others and increase a sense of autonomy and being in charge as she was clearly accustomed to being at home in the States. It didn't seem to chip away at the firm foundation of her self-consequence in the way it did Elinor or give her even a moment of self-doubt. Deborah felt perfectly at ease, speaking rather loudly and more distinctly in a kind of subject-verb English with the French teachers, as if by doing so they should be able to understand anything she had to say. Which is always very peculiar, because the French don't speak English.

Deborah recognized how difficult it might be, being so well versed in demonstrating proper concern for her child's education, by bossing the preschool teacher around with her firm grasp of child development under the handicap of a foreign language. But this feeling of being at the mercy of the generally ill-tempered French for a certain amount of understanding, patience and sympathy never bothered her. She refused to acquiesce to her weakness or ineptness in front of people whom she would normally disregard. It was hard enough to keep one's sanity in a country that didn't know what it was doing anyway. Because that's what it was— France didn't know what it was doing. Teachers, doctors, pharmacists, even toothpaste couldn't be trusted to know what it was doing, so why take the trouble? Why not claim the advantage of proficiency in the international language, the language of education, business and communication? Confirm to their faces the superiority of English as it dominated the planet and make *them* search out their high school English to communicate—hell if she was going to be the one to feel stupid, Deborah affirmed. Why couldn't Elinor summon up this audacity in the face of the beautiful Frenchwoman for example, with a *"ça va?"* and the slow, Indian chief English, accompanied by great pantomimic hand gestures. "SHE EATS," they would say, spooning some imaginary lunch from their other empty hand to indicate their child would eat in the *cantine* that day.

It wasn't that Deborah had little interest in Elinor because in fact she was very interested. She took note of nearly everything Elinor did, kept track and catalogued it in her efficient little mind as blatantly unconventional and despised her for her flagrant disregard for the rules. And Deborah had great respect for the rules and the literature that set them. All the baby manuals and child rearing guides she had read and followed as rigidly and with as much stamina as if she were training to swim the English Channel. She knew how to do things right—how to dress her children, what to read them, what methods of education were in vogue. She complained of the inadequacy of the school, but Elinor knew that when Deborah returned home to the States amongst her friends, she would boast of the superior education her girls had received at "private Catholic school in France."

Deborah dressed her girls in plaid dresses and smocked jumpers and shoes bought exclusively from well-known department stores like Saks and Lord & Taylor. Her girls never wore any of the plastic boots or velour skirts and flared leggings from the girls department at Eurodif or something Elinor might pick up for them at the supermarket. Deborah couldn't get back to civilization soon enough where people respected proper codes of conduct or at least were aware of them.

Elinor couldn't help notice that Deborah and her husband were trying a little too hard. "*Whoa,* slow down," she wanted to say, "no one's chasing you." Deborah did give the impression she was trying to catch up to a life that she thought she must have, one she had seen in a magazine or catalogue that looked more tempting than her own.

"Are you going up to the café for a coffee?" Deborah asked.

"Sure," Elinor agreed pleasantly.

The café was the place they could sit out on the streets of Cherbourg and amuse themselves with stories of their children, complain of their husbands, or more particularly, complain of the French.

The French could be difficult, very often unpleasant and even nasty at times. Elinor's earliest encounters left her with little emotion other than distaste. Victor had left her with her miserable high school French while he attended meetings in the States shortly after they arrived. When their freight container came with all their furnishings, the movers ignored most of what she said, although she had bought them each a six pack of beer to improve their spirits and extort a bit of effort on their part to assemble most of the furniture before they left her promptly at six o'clock standing alone with little Clara on her hip in a sea of cartons, books, and pieces of furniture lying about. She begged them to stay and assemble at least Clara's crib before they left.

"Mon mari va me tuer—my husband's going to kill me," she pleaded.

"What's he going to do? Fuck you to death?" the one with the long ponytail said in French to the great amusement of his friends and then they left her. Elinor supposed he never thought she would know what he meant. But although she understood the comment, she had nothing to say back. She felt angry, isolated—the most profound helplessness she had ever felt as a grown woman.

She felt like the optimistic American come to teach the world to sing. As Whitney Houston must have felt on her trip to France in the eighties—the lovely American girl, who had captured the world with her beautiful voice and came to France to share it. The French wanted it too and invited her to appear all over the television. And there she sat next to Serge Gainsbourg, the celebrated lounge lizard of the seventies, oily, shriveled and wan, with his famous cigarette hanging between his lips, visibly wasting from the fast and careless ill-treatment of himself in the pursuit of agreeable young women or *whatever*. His celebrity was based on little more than being outrageously *vulgair*, obnoxious and often disgusting. He had been married and chronically unfaithful to a beautiful British girl and said to Whitney Houston, in perfect English, which has gone down in French history as one of his most notable achievements, "I want to fuck you," on national French television.

"I do nothing but gain weight here in France," Karen Gaines said, munching a *torsade chocolat* with her *thé au lait*. Elinor watched her sweeten the coffee with a Nutrasweet pellet from her purse. She looked great—slim, blond and British, a Julie Christie at forty with three children, wearing leggings and an oversized sweater. "I've been trying Dante's diet—I eat, therefore I'm thin, but I ruin it every time because French pastry is not included in the equation. How do you do it, Elinor?"

"It's Descartes, Karen," Elinor said, sipping her petit café.

"Whatever. I don't know how you drink those things, although I'm sure they raise *your* metabolism, they just keep me up at night."

Hormone levels or the irrational concerns they had for their children kept them all awake at night, sweating with fear and guilt.

"It's what gives Elinor the hair on her chest," Deborah said, pulling Karen's compliment out from under Elinor with her well-intended malice. Deborah refereed their banter and made sure no one got too far ahead. There seemed to be some suggestion of desperation in the faint shadows of her face—the whisper of her anxiety was suppressed in her jovial repartee that rolled off her tongue as naturally as water off a duck's ass. But Elinor was familiar with the dreaded beast—the devil in the garden, Deborah was wild to keep at bay. It was the specter of dishar-mony, a desperate fear of singing and sounding off-key. And around Elinor particularly, Deborah appeared to be glancing around, looking for something familiar to grasp on to for support, some topic of conversation to ground her in the reality of which she belonged, not in the moral and social slumming she had to endure here in France. Deborah clung des-perately to the proper safety precautions that the French seemed to be unaware of, or at least ignored, like safety seats to age eight, (Elinor had heard it whispered that the Frenchwomen had been observed carelessly loading their children into minivans to simply roll around in the back like packages), proper nutritional snacks, scheduling her children's activ-ities, never allowing an idle moment where they might be forced to invent their own game. The French consider boredom an essential con-dition of childhood.

"Elinor thinks if she drinks enough of those *petit cafés* she might turn French," Deborah laughed.

"A horrifying consequence I suppose?" Elinor sighed. Sitting among these women she was bored. She was bloody bored, listening to the lives of her friends around the café table, making note of each other's successes and failures and comparing how each managed their husband and family.

"Where was Ruth last night?" Elinor asked.

"He doesn't let her go out you know. In fact she's never even had a babysitter for those kids. He just simply won't let her. He'll stay home with Stephen, but not with both of them. And if she says she wants to go out, he tells her not to bother coming home." Everyone gasped as if they had never heard of such threats. Girls night out—they were talking of girls night out. What was all of this about girls night out, anyway Elinor wanted to know, and what did they expect from it?

Stephanie Jacob walked up to the café with her beautiful blond toddler. She had just moved to France, and Deborah hurriedly pulled her up a chair at the table.

"Stephanie, I'm *so* glad to see you," she said, visibly relieved, and Stephanie took the seat, holding her little boy at the ends of her fingers between her knees. He stayed for a moment or two and then began to roam dangerously away, between the tables. Stephanie took from her purse a Ziploc bag of imported Pepperidge Farm Goldfish to lure him back and began popping them in the child's little pink opened mouth to keep him busy while she ordered her *chocolat*. Mrs. Jacob's house had once been featured in the home section of the local paper back home and that made her highly regarded in the community.

These women, wives and mothers, were as intent on seducing each other with their taste and domestic prowess as they had once been in attracting young men with their charms and allure in college. Deborah Knolls was perhaps the most practiced in this and leaned in and tucked her neat, smooth red hair flirtatiously behind her ear. She was dying to be admired, to inspire anyone to say, "*God,* she's beautiful, and her shoes, how can she be so together?" She had a late summer tan and an adorable light sprinkle of freckles across her nose that made her look positively pubescent, as if she were as young as one of the most sought after coeds on campus.

"Stephanie Jacob," she said pointedly, as if she were addressing a notable expert, "now you tell me, what is wrong with this house? It's only three hundred and fifty thousand?" She thrust a computer printout at her from her purse. Her prospects were never so bleak as Elinor's who would probably live in France forever.

Stephanie Jacob, being called on to give an important evaluation and her sought after opinion, began to say that indeed nothing was wrong with it and it looked positively charming and she was familiar with that particular subdivision and, to her, it appeared that Deborah had certainly found something worth looking at. France and the street side café receded to the background and the States and subdivisions came to the foreground. Deborah seemed to spend a good bit of her time at home, searching the Internet real estate pages for houses back in the States. The idea that she would have to endure the mediocre rental homes available in Cherbourg on such a long-term basis was an insupportable state of camping-out and living off canned goods, and she longed for nothing so much as to be a respectable homeowner again.

"Then why is it only three fifty?" she persisted.

"Well, some of the houses in that neighborhood just start at three fifty, that's all. It doesn't mean anything is *wrong* with it," Stephanie assured her.

Deborah had a funny look on her face as if she must be considering the idea of what it might be like to be in such a neighborhood but at the same time in the lower price range.

"Well, if you want a thirty-five-hundred square-foot all-brick, you pretty much have to look in that neighborhood," she said out loud to herself.

"I know of a house you can get for a song in Sterling Springs," Stephanie said.

"Really?" Deborah said with a little more enthusiasm.

"Yeah, Rachel Hampton moved into that neighborhood you know, and told me to get the word out for anyone who was interested."

"Oh," Deborah said in a haze of disappointment and envy that Rachel had moved home and into the fashionable world of such a high-priced neighborhood, "I know." Then Deborah hastened to assure the rest of the ladies not to make themselves uneasy. "It's nothing that great," she said. "You know, *new* money."

Hmmm, new money? Elinor thought. Isn't that what the bluebloods used to refer to the new wealth acquired in industry, and here they were the wives of engineers, accountants and salesmen using the term.

"And what does that make us?" she couldn't stop herself from asking, "*no* money?"

Deborah laughed and Karen, knowing nothing of the neighborhoods in the States, continued on about her insomnia.

"Lately, I can't sleep at all," she said, "and there'll be Nick snoring away like a baby. Men never have trouble sleeping. Sometimes I'll just stand by Nicola's or Sarah's bed at night and just watch them sleeping with a kind of envy for their worriless sleep that I never seem to get, even when I'm usually enormously tired. Some nagging guilt never allows me to yield to my exhaustion in the usual way I used to. Of course I'm always ready to fall asleep in the afternoon in an armchair, with the drool running down all over my book—never very peacefully, though. I always have this idea vaguely in the back of my mind that insists why bother when one of my kids will be waking me up any minute anyway."

"Or my husband," Elinor said. "It's been a week and the sexual tension is building. You know, that expectation that just hangs in the air between you in the evening. I go through the routine—pour myself a glass of wine and then pick out someone to imagine, like Denzel Washington for example. But lately you know what I've been fantasizing about?" She had everyone's attention now. Everyone was waiting.

"Furniture and appliances. I just bought a six hundred franc espresso machine and I swear, while we were making love last night I believe I was concentrating so hard, I was almost afraid I might shout out, Krupps! Krupps, yes! Yes! Yes!"

"Ooooh, Denzel Washington, Elinor?" Deborah said curiously.

"I love Denzel Washington. He's so heroic. Whenever there's a national crisis, like when the Twin Towers fell, I just thought, why not call Denzel Washington? He'll know what to do."

"For me it's Hugh Grant," said Karen.

Elinor was amazed. She never got the whole thing with Hugh Grant.

"Really?" she said with genuine curiosity. "That must be a British thing, because what is it with him that's supposed to be attractive? He's always being cast in these romantic roles as either the rakish cad or the darling boyfriend. And as a sexual fantasy, I cannot agree. I'd be afraid he'd be giving me that befuddled look the whole time."

"Well, I don't know *what* you're talking about," Deborah said devilishly. "Because it's never that way with *my* husband."

Deborah was joking of course, just for fun, but Elinor knew she couldn't pass up an opportunity to compare. Deborah was constantly measuring, and Elinor was amused by her comment, as if Phil Knolls, Deborah's husband, he could have been anyone, could be considered a sexual fantasy.

"I wouldn't give Elinor any ideas," Karen said.

Husbands! As if she would want Deborah's when she already had one of her own.

Deborah kept track of everything. Children were suppose to be potty trained and drinking from a cup by a certain age, and she could compare the French to none other than an inferior savage culture that allowed their children to enter preschool, still sucking from a bottle. All the American mommies were horrified by this practice. Not only was it embarrassing, it was clearly dangerous and irresponsible to the development of healthy teeth and certainly set the precedent for all the dental problems the French suffered from throughout their lives—another example of inferior personal hygiene, which was at the very core of civilized society. Elinor secretly enjoyed the more relaxed standards of personal hygiene.

Deborah could not comfort herself in any other way than to continually reassure herself that the French simply didn't know any better. And regarding Elinor, she could not summon these same feelings of pity, but rather could feel nothing but contempt for someone who knew better, but who consciously chose to disregard convention and common sense with a kind of open arrogance in favor of this unseemly enthusiasm she apparently had for France.

In France, Deborah Knolls was out there alone, brought up in her suburban world of church on Sundays for which to dress her children, company picnics, pool parties and Super Bowl gatherings to make it through the dreary months of her life and let her know she was doing okay. She baked cupcakes like a madwoman, decorated in every sort of theme—soccer balls, red, white and blue firecrackers, little pumpkin faces, or yellow chicks, bringing them to school activities, picnics and holiday gatherings in a basket, like Red Riding Hood, as if everything could be solved in a cupcake. But with every attempt to work her way on France, mold and shape it into something she recognized, Deborah grew increasingly bothered and agitated. How could one function in a world without structure and conformity, where no one understood the subtle differences between being vulgar, and being decent. And in France there was always the "issue of quality."

"Don't waste your money on the adorable little dresses in the shop windows for your children," she warned, although they were darling, she consented, they became unrecognizable after just one washing and practically fell apart.

"Who saw Jodie Foster on *TF1* last night?" Karen asked.

"I know, she's amazing. Her French is unbelievable. She did the whole interview in French!" Elinor said.

"You're kidding?" Deborah said.

"Didn't you see it?"

"No, we don't get French TV," she said.

"What do you mean, you don't get French TV?" Karen asked. "Is that even possible?"

"We only subscribe to British satellite. It's not like I'm going to watch French TV, anyway," she said matter-of-factly.

"Aren't you even a little curious?" Karen insisted, amazed.

Deborah ignored her, taking another sip of her *café crème*.

"Yeah, but do you think Jodie Foster could be that good, I mean don't you think they gave her the questions in advance so she could prepare?" Stephanie wondered.

"Well, you know, she *did* major in French lit, at Oxford, or something," Deborah assured everyone.

"I think it was Yale."

She was a genius, everyone agreed.

Ruth Kimbal walked up in her capri pants and stylish sling-backs, so unsuitable for the often dog-poop-soiled streets of Cherbourg, neatly coiffed and faintly trembling. France was such a shocking contrast to her life of tidy subdivisions and people with pleasant dispositions that the bringing of her children to school each day seemed to be a battle for her. Even her flawlessly highlighted hair, perfect manicure and expensive purse couldn't protect her from the possibility of an incomprehensible scolding or finger wagging from her child's *maîtresse* for waiting, holding the child's hand and not leaving him ruthlessly in the *Salle d'Accueil*—a chaotic room full of marginally supervised children, left to cope with their own miniscule understanding of the world or for some other thing she was not doing right. They were all terrified of not doing it right.

Ruth sank down in the chair next to Elinor rather defeated and said, "Sorry, but I had the misfortune to be held up by Madame Lambert."

About what? They all wanted to know.

"Well, you know Christopher isn't potty trained yet," Ruth admitted directly.

A hush fell over the group and no one spoke. Ruth had put her three-year-old in the *maternelle* wearing diapers? Ruth watched as a question was raised in the minds of each of the women around the café table as to her competence as a mother and realized immediately what she had done by announcing such a failure so openly. No one knew how to respond, how to encourage such a frank acknowledgement of her apparent negligence.

"Well," she stammered. "It was never like this with Alex or Campbell. Campbell trained in twenty-four hours," she said quickly, assuring the group that she was more than capable of accomplishing the task. But this only succeeded in directing the blame to Christopher, a grave error that only produced a silent sigh of relief that their own children had never shown such a deficiency and that *they* had never suffered such an embarrassment. Each felt a quiet satisfaction in their child's development and confirmation of their own abilities as a mother until Deborah said, "No big deal Ruth, my *husband* isn't even housebroken yet either." Perhaps she meant well, but in the end it simply sounded as if little Christopher were nothing more than a puppy.

3

Elinor drove to the city to pick up Alexi and Clara from school. As she approached the gate, she saw the beautiful Frenchwoman, standing with one booted foot up on the curb, her fine chin raised, as dashing as a country squire, wearing a field coat and jeans with a bright scarf at her throat. She was talking to Catherine Mort de Froy, a woman whose mere approach filled Elinor with dread. Catherine was American, but was married to a Frenchman, which made her believe she was the expert on being French.

She spoke perfect French and had accosted Elinor upon their very first acquaintance in such a direct and forward manner that assumed Elinor should be interested in everything about her and was now accosting the woman in the very same manner.

Catherine announced and proclaimed advice with such authority, as if she held a megaphone in her hand and was directing a chaotic group to order and discipline.

"*Les Americaines sourient trop.* Never smile at a Frenchmen unless you are prepared to suffer the consequences. As you can see, I made that error," she declared in her perfect French, informing the Frenchwoman that she had studied at La Sorbonne and had married a *banquier* in Paris. She overpronounced her French r's when she said, "we moved from P*a*r*i* to Cle*rrr*bo*uurrr*g two years ago, and people around here seem to think that means we have orgies every night because of it—Paris, you know." The woman smiled patiently, but was clearly appalled by Catherine's familiarity.

She had a master's in medieval literature and was close to a PhD, she continued, but got married and had children instead—two little girls who she hovered over like a bothersome insect. As she talked she kept turning to her little one playing nearby, announcing to her loudly, "mommy's right here *cherie*. She's just talking." She assured the woman that "she's okay, as long as she can see me." The child ignored her and seemed perfectly content in what she was playing.

"Elinor!" Catherine turned abruptly, away from the beautiful woman to ask if Elinor had voted for Bush, who was plainly responsible for all the embarrassing politics, so entertaining to the French.

"See, I knew it. It's the hair. You have great hair," she said, eager to conspire in their similar haircuts. Elinor was suddenly baffled and alarmed to be so drawn attention to in English, in front of the Frenchwoman. The little girl at Catherine's feet began to say, "Mommy, Mommy, Chloe has a bow, and, and, and, Mommy . . ." she was tugging on Catherine's slacks for her attention.

"*Oui, cherie*," Catherine said, removing the child's hands from her pants and smoothing them discreetly, saying how flagrantly stupid George W. was in English to Elinor, peppered with bits in French to fill the woman in on her worldly political view. Bush didn't even know where Bulgaria was, or the difference between Slovakia and Slovenia, can you imagine? How did anyone think he knew anything of the Middle East?

Elinor said nothing. The idea that Bush was uninformed, narrow-minded and inarticulate seemed so apparent it was ridiculous to act as if it required some particular perception of mind to discover. Elinor wished to say that he characterized the very self-satisfaction she noticed in the broad behavior of the other Americans come to live here—Catherine's own confidence in herself as one come to live among the French, married to a Frenchman even, with her charming ability in French. Her children, little Franco-Americans speaking their delightful *mélange* of English and French. It made Elinor ashamed of herself for no other reason than she wished to be so at ease in her situation, knowing how she was perceived by the culture at large—loud, arrogant and entirely insensible to the less fortunate nationalities. She listened to Catherine asserting her political views, lest she be thought typical, or equally grotesque. Elinor was suddenly irritated by the helplessness of her situation, her inability to have any influence on how her own country was perceived and had already secured how she should be.

"Mommy!" the child became more insistent. "Chloe has a bow, and, and, and she . . ."

"Does she *cherie*? That's called, 'conversational place holding,' " Catherine excused the child and then, to Elinor's amazement, translated the phrase into French, explaining that it was the technical child development term for interrupting. *"Elle veut tout simplement s'exprimer.* She just wants to have a place in the conversation." It was not uncommon to see a French mother in the market knock her child upside the head for interrupting, shouting, *"tu m'ennui!"* Literally, you bore me.

"Shhh," Catherine whispered, holding her finger to her lips, "you're interrupting mommy, and I better be quiet too, or I might offend some of the Southerners. I'm sure we're the only Democrats here," she affirmed. All Southerners were racist Republicans as stupid as Bush himself and undoubtedly his supporters. How else could he have gotten as far as he had in the way of ending up President of the United States? "Now, what was it you wanted to say, *cherie*?"

"Chloe wears a bow in *her* hair!" the child finally finished.

"Really? Does she? Because that's *great*. I love bows!"

Elinor could not suppress her profound embarrassment that they should meet like this, immobilized in fear that she would be called upon to defend her political beliefs in French which she did not feel prepared to do, and horrified that if she didn't, her viewpoint might be interpreted by *Catherine*, as if she couldn't speak for herself in French. She was suddenly envious of Catherine's facility in the language and her ease in expressing herself.

"*Elinor est pratiquement Européenne.* Her husband is Romanian," Catherine said, as if by being married to a socialist would demonstrate she was an exception to the rule and include her in their exotic sisterhood of enduring Latin mothers-in-law. That shared suffering alone could certainly bond the two of them in sisterly confidence for hours, Elinor thought jealously. Catherine rattled off in an eagerness to convey her proficiency in French that Elinor could not help but feel was peculiar to this woman who was expressionless, watching Catherine as if she were some incident, happening far off in the distance. The woman lit a cigarette and Elinor's breath caught in her throat. She almost couldn't breathe, it was so cool. It made Elinor kind of hate her, but she admired it just the same. It was so French.

"*Ca doit être pratique, alors*—that must come in very handy, Elinor, to have a husband who is Romanian in Europe," Catherine continued ecstatically in front of the woman. She seemed as eager to prove to the woman that she and Elinor were particular friends, as she was to show that Elinor couldn't possibly be as interesting to the woman as she herself must be. Catherine was aware of how the French viewed such barbaric cultures as the Romanians, who were recently quite unwelcome in France and were seen as poor gypsies from the east, sneaking across their borders and making untidy their grand boulevards in Paris.

"*Ah bon?* How is that?" Elinor asked.

"So that he can understand what the gypsies are saying before they snatch your purse on the Metro."

"*Ah, tout a fait*—Indeed," Elinor said flatly.

When the gates opened, the woman turned away as if she had never seen them before and Elinor looked down to watch her leather-booted foot step through the gate to receive her children from their teacher.

4

Europe is a paradise for the uncultured American whose palate is as uncorrupted as a toddler's that rejects such exotic fare as spinach and squash. What the American brings to Europe is wide-eyed innocence and a tenuous grasp of history. They are as captivated by it as they are repulsed by its sordid side. Their chaste, unspoiled minds are positively thrilled by the sight of wretched children in the street or the unsavory prostitute who waits in the dark, the hazard of dog shit on the streets or the waiter of obscure origin Elinor watches pee in the urinal, then stand at the mirror and run his hands through his greasy hair before he returns to his duties. Americans and the Brits have always amused themselves in the more primitive countries of Europe with pleasant climates at great inconvenience and sacrifice to their more sensitive tastes. By now Elinor felt some new connection and ease in the culture and could ask the waiter in the café for exactly what she wanted, flirt lightly with him even, but still felt very demanding to remind him he had forgotten her spoon. He might be amused by the American who spoke enough French to scold her about cutting her salad with a knife or not finishing her soup. She still never complained to find a hair in the *Pintade aux raisins*, deciding rather to enjoy the marvelous view and ignore the food, although it tasted divine.

In the twilight of the evenings, Elinor watched the tiny brown fruit bats dive and flutter like insects to feast on the fruit of the vineyard just behind the house. She watched the leaves turn lime green then yellow, red, orange and purple and drop off, leaving the twisted vines naked and black in the dampness. After the harvest, the *viticulteur* had insisted to her his vineyard produced the worst wine in all of Auvergne.

The days were turning cold and gray. She didn't mind. The gloom seemed to be part of the charm of her medieval village just outside of Cherbourg. The absurdity of a bit of bright green grass growing between the tire-worn road up to the vineyard struck her as so beautiful with an indifference to the cold and its own beauty that made her want to memorize it, never forget it, as she was constantly tracing the lines of the red tile roofed houses, and Romanesque geometry of the village church, reminding herself of what would always be her temporary enjoyment of this country. She knew the adventure of it would pass. Someday, she knew she would awaken and find herself back in the U.S. in a subdivision, driving a minivan, like a moving family room with air conditioning and TV—as if it had all been a marvelous dream. She dreaded the idea of eventually having to exchange a croissant for a Krispy Kreme. She already knew what her life would be. What was it about this land that was so mysterious and beautiful? Her house sat at the foot of Montluçon, the legendary plateau where the Gauls held off the Romans in 50 BC.

The American ladies visited the café less in the cold weather because Stephanie Jacob, who held some authority over the group, said she was deathly allergic to cigarette smoke, and they couldn't sit out in the street so much anymore. And no one with babies would actually go inside the carcinogenic café and expose their toddler to such toxic levels of second-hand smoke.

Elinor stopped to say good morning to the group of American ladies in the courtyard before dropping off the children with their teacher. Harriet Randall, dreadfully dull, plain in appearance and positively bleak in attitude, tired and uncaptivated by France, was saying how anxious she was to be home and "get on with her life." Her brother had e-mailed her all about the construction of his new house, "and here we are renting a house that's not home," she said through tears—she was given to weeping. "I just feel like our lives are on hold." Elinor stared at her and thought how she felt hers had just begun. Elinor's life seemed so much fuller in the way the French seemed to enjoy every part of it with such an unhurried pleasure that was as strange to her as it was delightful. Everything seemed more delicious, every moment celebrated with wine. The very ground she stood on seemed to contain so much secret knowledge and experience. She walked across the courtyard, trying desperately to disguise her distraction.

She had become entirely preoccupied with the Frenchwoman from the school. There was no doubt they noticed each other, and Elinor anticipated each encounter as she dropped off and picked up the children at school with an oddly familiar excitement she recalled from her youth—the same awkward palpitations that characterized youth itself and all its possibilities. And now she wished she could speak to the woman when she saw her. She was startled and alarmed enough by this keen interest to be slightly resentful of the woman's power over her.

The Frenchwoman was like nothing Elinor had ever seen before— like a heroine in a novel she had read when she was young and romantic. She had some forties Sophia Loren formidability that made her impossible to ignore the instant Elinor saw her. She pretended not to watch from behind her sunglasses, as the woman unloaded her children from her beat-up van, a dented old silver Renault Espace. She wanted to approach her and say, *"j'aime ta voiture!"* She felt she needed to say something to end the tension that seemed to exist between them or she might soon grow afraid of her. But instead, as they both stood awkwardly in the corridor together holding the hands of their little children, waiting for the teacher to appear, Elinor said, *"tu as ta fille dans la même classe que Clara. Je crois qu'elles sont copines.* Your daughter is in the same class with Clara. I think they're friends." She smiled, but as soon as the words were out of her mouth she fell back, *quelle horreur!* Elinor had *tutoyered* her! She had used *tu* instead of *vous*. It had seemed some familiarity existed between them to allow such a mistake, yet they didn't really know each other. The woman stared back at her with interest and responded politely, saying that yes, Elisabeth spoke a good deal about Clara at home while she was playing, pretending to read her books and talk to her in her play, she said. Elinor was thrilled and confused that the woman should know Clara by name.

Elinor knew that in France such familiarity is unacceptable between two people who have never been introduced. To assume that you know someone simply because you've noticed that their daughter is in the same class as yours is, quite justly, unforgivable. Although occasionally, if they feel like it, the French can excuse such an oversight simply because you are American and they understand that it is indeed easier to conjugate the verb or use *tu* or *ta*. And if they are sufficiently open minded or can be bothered to be so, they generally know that Americans are frightfully informal and casual and never think that behaving so is anything but charming and friendly. Americans are just so wide-eyed and ignorant with their universal goodwill that excludes no one and makes no distinction between acquaintances and intimate friends. They will discuss anything with the most casual of acquaintances—someone in the lobby of the gynecologist's office might learn what they are visiting him for. The stranger being so accosted might in turn share their medical history, without ever knowing their name. No one is considering if the other truly wants to be so informed. In fact, they behave nearly exactly the same to everyone and somehow this is considered sincere, open and, charming, not to understand the subtleties of being intrusive, or simply respecting the desire to be left alone. The French have a great talent for ignoring each other. Their language allows them to remove appalling people from their notice gracefully and eliminate any feelings of obligation that Americans find difficult to shake in a culture that values being friendly over intelligence or any kind of savoir-faire. *Voila la différence!*

The woman asked how long Elinor had lived in France, perhaps to acknowledge, or amplify that it was clear she was a foreigner and that either she understood her difficulty with the language, or had at least made note of it. Because the French feel no obligation to be pleasant or friendly, they have great difficulty being so even if they want to. Awkward silences don't faze them in the way they unnerved Elinor.

Desperate, Elinor finally commented on the obvious—that her two children must be twins. Yes, the woman acknowledged with a sigh to indicate her exhaustion, although she didn't appear so. She looked great—again with a pretty red scarf around her neck. Up close, the woman was startlingly handsome with a pale olive complexion and a broad face with high cheekbones. Her dark hair was loose to her shoulders and her brown eyes were flecked with gold, Elinor noticed, which gave her a curious charm. So provoking was her look that Elinor faltered under her gaze and looked away. The woman was so remarkable, her presence made her seem taller than she was and Elinor was suddenly indignant—she did not think that she liked women who were more beautiful than she was.

"It is especially difficult with four children in a small apartment in the city," the woman continued. Elinor said that she hoped Clara was speaking French with them and the woman turned to her little girl, "*Elisabeth, Es-ce que Clara parle bien Français?* Does Clara speak very good French?" The little girl nodded up and down in exaggerated approval.

They were presently saved by the appearance of the teacher and were spared any further exchanges that might reveal a certain bold curiosity in each other.

That evening, when Elinor and the woman ran into each other picking up their children, they pretended they had never seen each other before. Primarily Elinor, because in her culture it seemed rude, but in France it was so natural that Elinor almost believed the woman truly hadn't ever seen her before.

The next day, as Elinor was urging Alexi to go to school, Alexi was in one of her moods and could not be persuaded, she turned to see the Frenchwoman approaching, walking across the courtyard toward her in her wonderful unhurried way, so careless and relaxed that it conveyed a perfect satisfaction and comfort in her body. In the instant that Elinor turned to see her, she could see the outline of the woman's breasts, the roundness of her belly and the swell of her lovely hips from beneath her loose sweater, swaying toward her as if in stop-action photography—each image seared her brain. The woman was not hard or taut like her. Elinor was all hard angles and muscles. She had no softness or luxury. Instead Elinor had relentlessly pounded off any traces of postpartum flesh that audaciously lingered after her two children with a kind of fearful dread of becoming dowdy, dumpy, or worse—invisible. There was something helpless and hopeless in a woman whose appearance inspired so little interest that she might as well be invisible, and Elinor dreaded her inevitable loss of power. Her inescapable transformation from smart, sexy, woman-in-her-prime, to stout suburban housewife and mother, frightened her onto the treadmill in the garage. Elinor had never been able to carry off those extra pounds that made the Frenchwoman look even more beautiful and comfortable in the soft-focus life Elinor was sure this woman had. Exercise, it seemed, would never suit her perfect comfort in having four children, Sunday dinners, and evenings on the sofa with her husband.

The woman approached her directly, even though Elinor, recovering herself, quickly turned away and tried to sooth Alexi's whining that she wouldn't go to school. But when Elinor looked up, the woman gave her a lazy appraisal and a faint smile of recognition, but said nothing, meeting Elinor's curious stare with such frank directness of an unmistakable intensity that suggested she knew and understood her perfectly. An appreciative, direct assessment—a kind of sizing up, a satisfied look of approval—that made Elinor uncomfortable and embarrassed. She looked away momentarily and then said weakly, "and your children are so very well behaved," only she said, *bien enlever* instead of *élever,* which meant, *very well taken off with*, or perhaps *kidnapped*. She supposed she could have said *bien laver*—well washed—but she didn't. She was sure the woman must think she was crazy anyway, and she looked quickly away as if ashamed, like she had been found out, her admiration for the woman discovered. She went on coaxing Alexi to her teacher, self-conscious of her English in front of the woman's notice. How did she know? For it was shocking how directly the woman had demanded an exchange of looks, insisting some mutual inclination existed between them.

Elinor turned away and tried to ignore her. She pretended she didn't even notice the woman's look of comprehension that was as captivating as it was unnerving. Clearly she understood Elinor's curiosity in her—her attraction, infatuation even. Elinor remembered how they had noticed each other to begin with. She remembered how she was struck by the woman picking up little Elisabeth and carrying her effortlessly on her shoulders. It seemed so wonderful, masculine even, self-sufficient, and capable in a way she had never encountered in another woman. So entirely out of character for what Elinor generally knew of these cool elegant creatures on the playground—the other French mothers, so delicately feminine, they even spoke with a higher pitch to their voice than her unrefined, frank openness. Her own American voice had none of the delicacy of their tinkling chatter.

Each day the woman approached the gate to pick up her children, smoking a cigarette, they met each other's gaze. In fact, they always met each other's gaze directly. "That woman is staring at me," she thought, astonished really. The woman seemed to demand her attention, nearly every day in the courtyard and then pretend not to notice when Elinor stared back with curiosity, for indeed it was a curious thing for a woman to do. What did the woman know of her? What did she think, Elinor thought with indignation, that with her bold familiar friendliness, she was trying to come on to her, she realized with a sudden rage. And it was clear that this might never have occurred to her but in France. France with its ambiance of flirtation that was everywhere. She felt it all around her—the food, the fashion, even the demitasse of coffee she sipped at the café with the other ladies was richer in flavor, darker in color and thicker. The sliver of *chocolat* that sat on the saucer beside it was black and bitter, an assault to the senses that evoked both pleasure and pain. Everything was stronger, bolder and more obvious. People smelled different, more pungent, and alive. Cigarette smoke thickened the air, and everything was bodies and moisture. On the coldest of days you could be sure to be sweating in the close confines of a café heated by bodies and discussion. Elinor seemed to always be vaguely aware of the immediate sexual tension present in every ordinary encounter—a trip to the dentist, or hairdresser, the look of the *boulanger*, handing her his long baguette, asking the butcher for particular cuts of meat—legs, breasts, thighs. It all seemed overwrought with suggestion. Why shouldn't the woman think she was coming on to her when clearly she was attracted. What other interpretation could the woman possibly have of Elinor's interested behavior besides a sexual overture—it seemed a very natural thing in a country where they were so skilled in seduction, yet so inept at something so banal as friendship. The advertising of the most mundane products, laundry detergent, yogurt, shoes, the sensual curves of steam rising from an advertised cup of coffee used this very understanding of the universal weakness for the whisper of sex.

It was clear the expatriate community was swept up in it as well. They all insisted on socializing together regularly, and the exotic location had everything to do with encouraging a more permissive atmosphere. They were quick to adopt the French custom of kissing each other on each cheek in the friendly and chic manner of the French. But for simple Americans, unused to the exotic custom of casual kissing, it quickly became an excuse to kiss each other's husbands and for the men to kiss other men's wives. Americans seem to have a gift for misinterpreting the cultures of others, and one could see how the custom could be easily abused. After being married for nearly ten years, perhaps they all entertained the idea of love affairs with their girlfriend's husbands. This was no great confession to make, as married men and women do it all the time—flirt with each other. Elinor remembered how it sometimes left her breathless, the implications of some of these innocent flirtations. It seemed so forbidden and dangerous to play these games with other women's husbands.

Elinor decided to hate the woman. That evening she walked right past the woman's designated spot on the playground that she wanted to mark with a big piece of sidewalk chalk and didn't give her a second glance.

"Here," she wanted to say as she drew a big white X, "this is your place." The woman was like a goddamned chess piece—the queen, capable of moving stealthily anywhere, all over the board. The woman would stand in front of Clara's classroom blocking Elinor's way it seemed, waiting for the twins to appear. Once she had noticed the woman however, it was very hard to unnotice her, and Elinor watched the twins playing in circles around her, often agonizingly with Clara, while she waited for

Alexi to be let out from the primary school. But her efforts were in vain, she couldn't avoid her, it was like she was everywhere, on purpose, Elinor suspected. Elinor came up behind her to wait for Clara, there was no place else to go, and when the woman bent to pick up Elisabeth, Elinor watched her hair fall across her face in the most maddeningly beautiful way that filled her with a longing she did not know.

5

On Friday, Elinor was late. She pulled up to the sidewalk on the street in front of the school and opened the car door, only to practically slam it into the woman, or knock one of her children to the ground as they walked up the narrow sidewalk. They reluctantly acknowledged each other and Elinor let her pass before she helped Alexi and Clara out of the car and up the sidewalk to the school. She let Alexi run up ahead to her class with her Christmas package for her teacher and then entered the chilly corridor to wait for Clara's teacher. There was the Frenchwoman, standing with the twins. Elinor didn't even look at her, determined to prove she had no designs on her. She just stood silently, waiting as if they were as anonymous as strangers waiting for the bus. She stood in determined silence, squeezing Clara's hand till she twisted it out of her grip.

Other parents gathered. They both in turn politely said "bonjour" to each one as they entered. To neglect to say "bonjour" can only be interpreted as rudeness. As children, the French are taught to always greet each other with "bonjour." However, each time Elinor said it to one of the other parents seemed only to emphasize the fact that they had not said it to each other. Minute after minute passed, and a harsh feeling of regret began to emerge with a great force that immobilized Elinor even further into unmoved determination to ignore the woman, although she began to need a way to reverse her foolishness and to have walked in with a smile and a "bonjour."

This would never have happened in the States. If they spoke the same language, had the same culture, she would have easily ended the tension by saying something like, "this is silly, I believe there has been some mis-understanding. I'm Elinor, Clara's mommy and Clara would love to have Elisabeth come over for lunch one day." Even if she never followed up on it, that is what she would've said to end this excruciating tension. She was always saying things like that to other mommies in the States, just to be friendly and acknowledge the little friendships between their children.

Although the more Clara and Elisabeth were struggling to play together, Clara peeping and waving to her from between Elinor's legs, the more obvious was their refusal to acknowledge one another, although Elinor couldn't face the friendship between them and the ultimate, unavoidable and uncomfortable connection she would have with Elisabeth's mother.

When Clara's teacher appeared, Elinor made the hand-off, turned away and ran up the stairs to see if Alexi had gotten to her classroom, feeling some catastrophic loss for what she had done. She had snubbed the one person she wished desperately to know. Elinor saw that Alexi was alone in the hall. Her *cartable*, hat, coat and mittens were on the floor, and she was busy by the trash can with her Christmas present for her teacher. She was tearing off the card and trying to throw it away.

"What are you doing Alexi?" Elinor heard herself squeal it as if she were in pain. Although Alexi had picked out the present herself, she had watched Elinor write the card, a sort of funny thing—a Season's Greetings and Happy New Year little card with a drawing of a lively fat woman holding up a glass of champagne for a toast. She had used it because she had run out of the *Joyeux Noël* ones with Madonna and Child. Alexi had been rather disappointed by the idea of it Elinor could tell and asked why she couldn't have one like the one she had written for

Clara's teacher. Elinor explained that she had run out, feeling impatient with Alexi's constant dissatisfaction. She didn't have another like the others, she explained, and she needed to just be done with the task and have it wrapped and ready for her to bring to school the next day before school was out.

"No," Elinor said, "you have to give that to your teacher. Alexi," she pleaded, "you have to give that to your teacher, or she won't know who it is from, and Mommy wrote it to tell her thank you for taking care of you," she said in her more reasonable voice, although there was a singing buzz in her ears, the result of the painful regret for what she had done just moments before in the corridor.

Children have the uncanny ability to sense the shattered nerves of their mother, or the upset of the usual calm that Elinor tried to maintain over the family, and will always take full advantage of the situation, behaving like little beasts, particularly, it seemed, when Deborah Knolls might be an audience to it. Elinor looked quickly around to catch Deborah's expression of satisfaction that her children never behaved in such a manner.

"Alexi, you're embarrassing me. You're embarrassing Mommy," she whispered, instantly regretting it. Because she knew she would pay for it later. Anytime Alexi was frustrated with something she was doing or making, Elinor heard her say, "Mommy, I can't do this. This jump rope is embarrassing me," or "I can't make this," using far too much Scotch tape than was necessary to attach paper wings to a toilet paper roll. "These butterfly wings are embarrassing me." It was the echo of her mother's frustration that Elinor thought sometimes meant *I can't do this—I'm embarrassing me, I'm not a very good mommy.*

"But she won't like it," Alexi said, her beautiful brown eyes filling with tears.

"Why?" Elinor asked, trying to understand in her state of confusion. She squatted down and was holding her by the shoulders.

"Because. Because it's funny. She'll think it's silly."

Elinor took the card from her.

"You give her the gift, Alexi, and I'll tell her thank you," she said finally, feeling so utterly sad and defeated herself, as this child was so capable of making her feel. Alexi's sensitivity tortured her, she had a way of allowing everything to crush her so completely that instead of being sympathetic, her awkwardness rose up like some nightmare from Elinor's past, and she was overwhelmed by it. It often made her angry, rather than feeling pity. Elinor understood the injustice of having such a graceful, perfect little sister, and for a moment she disliked even her lovely child Clara for being so perfect and good.

"Oh, for heaven's sake child, no tears," Elinor said, fairly pushing Alexi into the classroom, feeling guilty for how she knew she punished her, never directly, but always in her disregard, a look, her giving up and walking away from her so she could cope. She began to understand and feel deeply Alexi's frustration, and it was the worst kind of punishment— a deep feeling of discontent. Elinor would crawl into bed with her at night and stroke her beautiful hair and whisper how much she loved her, although it was never enough. She sensed Alexi understood the inadequacy of her words, thought that her mother was as beautiful, distant and cold as her teacher and that the words she spoke were simply that— words. She clung to her, wishing they were real. It wasn't fair that Clara got all her patience and tolerance—it was as if she wanted to love up all her babyness before it was gone, and Alexi got nothing but all her expectations and disappointment.

She tried to deny her fault in Alexi's behavior and vowed to devote herself to her more completely, and not forsake her beautiful child's love. For indeed Alexi was lovely, like Victor, who she had married mostly for his beauty. Alexi had the same dark gypsy beauty that she was so struck by in Elisabeth's mommy. But despite her perfect loveliness, she could not charm or beguile in the same way Clara could.

Elinor came home crying, pitying herself—miserable mother and foolish idiot. What was the matter with her? Did she imagine herself in hopeless love with the woman? A woman! It was absurd! What was it she wanted? To be her for a day, so cool and aloof? To inhabit her skin—*être bien dans sa peau*, to be so much like her, so indifferent and French? What must it be like to be so beautiful, to think, to speak in French? Did Elinor envy her life that she had conjured up in her imagination while she stood at the kitchen counter, sipping coffee, watching her children eat their breakfast? She felt desperate, foolish and ashamed as if she were the only person in the world who had ever fallen in love. Because she knew this agony of desire was called love—that she was in love with a *woman*, a stranger. The perversity, the implausibility of it shocked and repelled her and still intensified her desire. She wept the wretched tears of a child. *Oh, Alexi,* she cried, *would that you had a better mommy, one who was less miserable, vulnerable to such a childish crush.* She sobbed.

Even as a little girl, Elinor remembered thinking that it was the boys who were truly beautiful—arresting and eye-catching—more aesthetically pleasing than women. She looked at paintings in her art history classes as a young woman in college and thought the same thing. It was the men who were beautiful, well-formed and muscled. Women were lush and untidy—slovenly even. She looked at the large copy of Albrecht Durer's *Adam and Eve* which hung in her living room, and it was clearly Adam who drew the eye, not Eve. How could she be so taken with this woman? And yet it was all her lush femininity that was so intoxicating. She imagined. She pictured the woman's pale face, her heavy brunette hair, her throat she trembled to touch with trepidation. The image became clear in her mind so that she could see her perfectly, every detail of her, the look in her eyes that she met nearly everyday. What was in that look? She demanded to know. She watched the image of the woman in her mind, the heave of her breasts and the sweet swell of her lovely hips bend to pick up one of her children. She would go mad, she thought.

The problem was her life was far too easy. Staying at home, looking after the children, keeping them safe and in well-fitting britches, keeping them in juice, lunch, tape, Band-Aids, crayons and paint was often not enough. They required much more than that and they did not deserve this great distraction she had entertained in her head during these last weeks.

In a panic, she called her mother and lied to her that she needed her to make an appointment with a therapist or psychiatrist on their trip home to the States for Christmas. It was really her only chance of getting an appointment, if she wanted to speak to a doctor in English. She told her mother that it was because she and Alexi were not getting on that well lately, and she needed some coping skills. She said she had thought about it a long time and needed her to make her an appointment right away. She had thought to do it here in France, but knew that her French was still inadequate to really discuss things as complicated, as herself for instance, or her relationship to her daughter and other things that she didn't even understand, or feel adequate to express in her own proper *langue*. Her mother bought it and was very understanding because, of course, Elinor assured her a hundred times, not to think she was crazy or desperate. The last thing a mother wants to hear from her grown-up daughter is that the real reason she thinks she needs to talk to a shrink is because she's in love with a woman.

Now, this really wouldn't be that big of a deal if it was something quite normal and acceptable in today's modern-thinking, enlightened, liberal-minded and open society, like a kind of latent sexual awakening, as Elinor was sure the capable and qualified clinical psychiatrist who her mother would make the appointment with would say, or in terms very similar, she imagined. But that wasn't it. It was much more complex than that and *surtout*, she was not a lesbian and she was certainly not latent.

Her mother reassured her she didn't think she was crazy and that it was really quite understandable she should want to talk to someone when she was safely back in the States. She always imagined Elinor to be crazy anyway to want to leave the safe haven of the United States, so tidy and convenient, where air-conditioning, walk-in washers and dryers large enough for any ordinary-sized family load that could be operated simultaneously without blowing a circuit, and peanut butter abounded. Her mother soothed her by saying that problems tended to exaggerate themselves by being isolated in a foreign country and that she would make the appointment right away.

Elinor hung up the phone and began to think of how she might explain to the doctor what had happened. Where might she begin to recount to this doctor, in his ordinary life of listening to the anxieties and problems of the family lives of the citizens of Normal, Illinois, that she had fallen in love. What would she say? That in her crazy world of convenience and luxury, when the neurosis of the modern woman is as commonly accepted as some rather annoying inconvenience, or redundant interruption like a sales call, or that idiotic thing you get when calling a place of business that tells you to respond to several options by pressing a number on your touchtone phone, that she fell in love with a woman in her spare time, in her imagination, while she did the laundry, cleared the table, dressed the children, while she chopped the onions and put them in the sauce, sipping delicately on a glass of Bordeaux. Bordeaux, not zinfandel, or some California merlot or perhaps something white and chilled that was popular to drink with women like herself who shared her similar circumstances and tax bracket in the States.

What would she say? How would she start? She was an artiste, a painter—amateur, of course, she would say, to give herself some occupation and raison d 'être for her madness. Inspired by all the beauty that surrounded her in France, she had started painting in the garage—large, cartoonish copies of Botticelli, Van Gogh and Michelangelo. If you could call a thirty-six-year old mommy who has no other specified daily duties other than to take care of her children—wash, dress, and present them well at school and be naturally concerned with their health, nutrition, and welfare with the added luxury of a good bit of time in between—an artist.

No, perhaps not an artist, a collector of art, or an appreciator of art and beautiful things. Like the rest of the *true* appreciators of art who swarm Europe, whom she noticed in many of the museums and restaurants they visited throughout their travels, who always regarded her with annoyance, while she interrupted their *true* appreciation of the food, wine or art, with her children and backpacks, strollers, maps, guides, snacks and toys and most horrifying of all, loud explanations to the children, interrupting their quiet contemplation while gazing at some spectacularly famous work of art like Botticelli's the *Birth of Venus* for example.

"She's naked, mommy," little Clara would giggle.

"Of course she is naked sweetie," Elinor would instruct with authority, more for the benefit of the art appreciator than for Clara.

Clara would look at her in confusion.

"Well, she *was* just born," Elinor would further explain.

Clara was not convinced.

"Well, do you think *you* were fully clothed when you were just born?" she would finish sheepishly, turning the stroller and moving away to the next great work of art.

Elinor probably couldn't even classify herself as an appreciator of art—although she did minor in art history. Beauty overwhelmed her, although she could speak about it in casual conversation as a generally benign thing. She was easily overwhelmed, indeed "overstimulated, if I may, *doctor*, say it in terms that I am sure are familiar to you in your profession," she would say. She was overstimulated—fascinated by beauty and a kind of a pervasive curiosity that when all the scissors and crayons, wayward socks and shoes, Barbies with their dresses pulled up over their heads were put away, in her heart strange desires arose.

"You see, I live in France," she would explain. Here, he might interrupt her and begin to say that he has visited there on his vacations, as people often do, particularly doctors, who she often visited for checkups for the children while she was home in the States. But she would quickly interrupt him before he began to tell her about Provence. After all, she has perhaps only an hour or so to talk to him. Although, as she begins to unfold her story, it occurs to her how good it is when she says to him, "I fell in love with a woman."

After it comes out of her mouth in such a frank and matter-of-fact statement of the truth, she observes his apparent interest and attention change. He is indeed surprised, but hardly disappointed. Clearly, he didn't expect *this* from his nine o'clock. She has little idea of what problems or anxieties the bulk of his patients bring to him each day. But she sees in an instant they are normally not this good. She has never been able to contain her enthusiasm for all the possibilities life presents except through physical exertion and often denial. Hell, she was in better shape than Madonna, and why shouldn't she be when her luxurious life made it possible? It also kept the specter of age at bay for her as if she were constantly training for some event she felt certain would require all her strength and stamina.

She did not always possess this allure. And, in fact, was quite awkward as an adolescent and young adult. Her coltish (a ridiculously flattering term for what was more often clumsy and ungainly) long limbs were never as desirable as the more well proportioned and shapely legs of her peers in high school. More often they were the source of shame and embarrassment. She would begin to tell him a bit about her tomboyish youth as isn't that certainly what she was paying him for?

It was true, however, that as a child, she never paid any attention to the fact that perhaps she didn't receive the same type of attention pretty little girls did, but perhaps she wouldn't have wanted it. She never liked to be fussed over, or paid much attention to, so the idea of being beautiful, or desirable as a woman was entirely novel to her. But she did enjoy being beautiful. Or was it ultimately tiresome? Was it really worth the effort? But without her looks, she would be meaningless and have no influence on the world.

As a child, she had deplored the idea of dresses, dolls, playing house, seeming to recognize early the idea of "house" as confined and unvarying, lacking the element of adventure she seemed to always be searching for. Although wasn't that what she was playing now? House?

She was always possessed of a certainty and uncommon sense, startling perhaps in a child, particularly an ungainly child. People are always excusing odd or indeed obnoxious behaviors in pretty little children, but are much less tolerant or perhaps even alarmed by precocious little girls who have no reason to behave in any other way than might make up for what they lack in beauty.

She despised baths, brushing her hair or cleaning her toenails. She was the last of five children, so her mother was tired enough to let her have her way. But around puberty, her infrequent bathing habits and physically active life of running after a pack of neighborhood boys her brothers ran with unfortunately came to an end.

They built a clubhouse out of scrap wood, painted it camouflage to conceal it, and hung *Playboy* magazine pictures of naked girls on the walls. "No girls allowed!" was painted on the door in red paint. But no one considered her a girl anyway, so she was accepted immediately without much consideration. But her acceptance by this pack of savage boys did not lessen the blow of discovering that even her ungroomed appearance wasn't enough to disguise her femininity.

By the sixth grade, some of the more bold ones were asking her to the movies, something she mistook for being just another thing to do with their pocket money on a hot summer afternoon, but which surprised her by being an opportunity to practice their romantic yearnings on someone who didn't really count, someone who was completely non-threatening, oddly familiar, not so strange and mysterious as *real* girls who you sat next to in math class and tried to smell. You could smell Elinor easily without even trying, and yet she was still, technically a girl.

Her friend Burt, who was two years older than she and in another class so she hardly ever saw him at school, frightened her nearly out of her seat at the movies and out into the blinding July sunlight by reaching over to her in the dark and fumbling his greasy hands under her T-shirt for her small breasts on her otherwise boy's body. Unused to the fact that she even had breasts, at first she thought he might be trying to wipe the popcorn grease off on her T-shirt and was about to tell him to "cut it out and use your own T-shirt," but when she turned to whisper it meaning-fully, she saw his large face looming toward her, eyes closed and mouth open. She gasped in horror and shoved him as hard as she could back into his own seat.

"What the hell are you doing, Burt?" she shrieked in the dark.

"Nothing," he hissed through clenched teeth. Their other friends were twisting around in their seats to see what was going on.

"What are you doing?" they asked, giggling. "Are you making out with Elinor?" they hurled at Burt in disgust and disbelief. It was almost as if he had tried to kiss one of *them*. Burt hated her after that, and she hated him, too. It wasn't merely the fact that he had tried to kiss her, but he had revealed to the rest of the group that she was a girl. Elinor would never forgive him for that. She was never fully accepted by the group again, and by high school, she stopped running with them entirely.

But as a woman, what was once ungainly and boyish, Elinor carried off with elegance and style in their contradiction. Most importantly, her boyish beauty was fashionable. And everyone knows that fashion is not always beautiful, and what is truly beautiful is not always fashionable. And perhaps she simply had an enormous vanity and very little beauty, but little is required for a woman to become a heroine in a novel other than to be beautiful and to find herself in extraordinary circumstances.

Beauty is always being misunderstood as pride, although it is true, a beautiful woman always imagines herself to deserve something more, to be the object of the desire of others. And naturally, a beautiful woman is always casting herself in romantic roles and intrigues which she concocts for herself in her head. That's why it's always easy to understand, for example, why *Doctor Zhivago's* Lara, or Madame Bovary, Anna Karenina or Hester Prynne all cheated on their husbands. Because a beautiful woman always fancies she should be made love to. And all of this she might have told him, but for a brilliant, almost blinding revelation that this man's tiny viewpoint and meager clinical training could never comprehend what she suddenly saw as a marvelous and strange as it was unlikely, love affair that in that instant she decided to embrace as extraordinary, instead of having him classify it as some neurosis, possibly prescribing her medication. Perhaps she did have a problem. She had spent her life being something she couldn't even satisfy, much less fall in love— with a woman? Was it so absurd? She had never been very much distracted by the usual nonsense that the world has always gobbled up, or been gobbled up by. Nothing particularly significant other than the usual social tangles that begin at such an early age that she witnessed her six-year-old crushed by already. The harsh reality of these conflicts was usually based on nothing more than who has Super Day-Glo Barbie or such. She wanted to be able to tell Alexi that it gets better later in life. But sadly, she knew it didn't. Grown-ups were still vying for who gets to be the mommy and boss everyone around, or who gets to be the most sparkly princess and have thousands of otherwise unemployable young men, knocking each other over to take her photograph.

These webs of woe usually reached their peak of importance in high school and then continued to degenerate throughout the rest of adult life, causing either exaggerated feelings of self-consequence entirely removed from any true sense of taste or intelligence, or quite the opposite, leaving enormous scars of self-doubt, crippling them for life. And all of this childish rubbish is proved to be of great interest and importance to the bulk of the population by the popularity of magazines to be found in enormous quantities in the waiting rooms of the pediatrician's office, or at the hairdresser's and consumed by the public as if the very secrets of life might be revealed in the goings on of persons who might as well have been Krista Cunningham, homecoming queen of Hillcrest High School 1982. "Or who is really popular now, you know, is Cindy Crawford who was in my chemistry class at Northwestern," Deborah would say. It is always important to have had some contact, some shared experience, like having sat in an enormous lecture hall with someone like Cindy Crawford. "She's *darling*, she really is."

The idea that this marvelous love she felt would be certainly misinterpreted, rationalized, diagnosed or even talked of to some doctor, peering curiously at her over his glasses, who she had been referring to as "him," but who, worse could be a *her—a lady shrink*, who would examine her like some squirming specimen, sprawling on a pin, with compassion and sisterly confidence, prescribing her Xanax or some other kind of pills to calm, or even more desirable, *kill* her overwrought emotions and send her happily medicated and on her way, back into her life that should normally be in a quiet shady subdivision with a name like Darling Heights or Fervent Meadows, happily tying bows into the matted synthetic hair of a Barbie doll, filled her with such dread that she picked up the phone and called her mother back and said she was fine, and simply in a moment of panic and temporary self-doubt. Elinor assured her she was a competent mother and that she couldn't talk right now because they were just leaving for the park. What could a psych major possibly know about discovering a fascinating new culture? Elinor fell in a pathetic heap on the bed in the chill of the house, pulled the comforter up over her and slept.

6

She opened her eyes in the gloom of the bedroom. She had pulled the *volets* closed to shut out the early December sun and darken the room. She would have to pick up the children from school in an hour, but she didn't want to face the unpleasant climate of the cold room. The lonely reality of her role and the responsibilities that went along with it—being a wife and mother, being herself besieged her, and she dreaded having to perform the role she played, rather unconvincingly she was afraid and she was exhausted by the performance they rehearsed in front of each other, or in front of their husbands even, pretending that they knew what they were doing, when really it was a mad world she roamed in adrift. She was not nervous, or afflicted as other women were, depressed, or suicidal, confining herself to her bed, room nineteen, or the attic, susceptible to mad fits in general protest to the role of her sex and all the domestic and sexual duties associated with it. The school gate was merely the curtain to the stage that lay beyond in the courtyard, in the realization of the farce of their lives. And one could be sure Deborah Knolls took it very seriously, like some ruthless casting director who called out, "Hey, you in the leg warmers. You're out!"

Even Elinor was afraid of her. She had heard her announce one day that Betsy Kincaid had embarrassed the whole American community by wearing shorts and flip-flops last summer to pick up her kids, exposing her pudgy knees to ridicule without any thought as to how it might effect the rest of them. Grown women in France did not wear shorts.

Elinor had never felt adequate to the task of being an adult, much less a mother, responsible for the raising of little people. Let's face it, it was time to give up those childish dreams. She would never be Lady Diana, or even Deborah Knolls who seemed to command motherhood with as much precision as she vacuumed the living room rug, passing her upright vacuum (the French canisters were much too awkward and ineffective) in straight and perfect strokes so that when she stood alone in the house at the periphery, a faint smile of satisfaction curled her lips, and she marveled at the beauty and symmetry of the lines in the carpet. When the peasants stormed the Bastille, Deborah would be banging at the gates of Versaille screaming, "But, it's *me!* I have the right shoes and purse!"

Even if she did wear the right shoes, Elinor would never be one of those romantic mommies enjoying something like a latte while she sat on the porch swing, watching her angelic children dressed in Ralph Lauren playing in the shady yard. It never happened like that. Those kids, although very likely to be dressed in Ralph Lauren, were more likely to be playing XBox next door in the cool of the air conditioning. Even Lady Diana could hardly have been expected to be herself—there was too much pressure. She felt the pressure of her own silly life as she looked at her defeated expression in the mirror. The face that stared back at her, she began to resign herself to the idea, was more than likely the face, swollen from crying, she would see for the next ten years.

But none of them were getting any younger. She thought of the faces of the other mommies on the playground, the American women, so wearied by the constant battle they faced raising their children up against a foreign culture that made even the easiest routine tasks of signing their children up for fencing or understanding their child's progress at school, an enigmatic and daunting experience. They complained of the brutality of the playground that their children had to face every day. It wasn't fair. The savage French children would never share the soccer ball, or allow other kids to get in the game. And the teachers stood idly by, making no effort to impose any kind of moral justice, order, or common courtesy on the savage playground.

It is inevitable that a woman so much in charge of everyone else neglects herself and is rarely considered important other than for the pleasure and accomplishment she inspires in others. Strange desires are perhaps the result. The vastness of the possibilities is distant and impossible, and only the faint music of their song teased and tormented her. Elinor was bound to the house very often and to its duties, and she understood the necessity of it, knew that her friends as well as the handsome Frenchwoman suffered from the confinement of their duties. Indeed it would be silly not to concede that all of them would willingly shed their role in exchange for youth, passion and love. But there was always the house, which would seem such a pleasant place, and it was—in the moments that she had it to herself. In the mornings, before the sun came up, before her husband reached for her and before the little voices called for her. She would savor the silence with jealous contentment, before it would be ruined by her husband. Her sweet, sweet husband with his Labrador-like devotion. It was all rather disappointing or banal. Elinor wished she could feel more affection toward his hand moving purposefully for her thigh under the covers. Victor would pull her to him and nuzzle her neck with such thorough confidence and assurance, as if she were as comforting and familiar as Clara's blanket, and it made Elinor stifled and cross. Men were so tiresome, not practical men like Victor necessarily, but intellectual men, like Philip Roth. Nothing was ever so boring as a man who thought himself brilliantly interesting. And she could at least be satisfied that it was simply her husband reaching for her and not someone who fancied himself a genius. But there was something fascinating and inexplicable in the idea of a woman.

She made herself a pot of coffee and hoped it might lift her spirits and forget the possibility of the Frenchwoman, so elusive and *soi-distante* from her now. The dim afternoon sun was bleak in contrast to the magnificent landscape beckoning her to enjoy it and all that was wonderful in France.

She walked up to the school gate to stand in the huddle of American ladies, in cloth coats and leather gloves. Deborah Knolls walked up in a smart new black leather jacket. It clashed dreadfully with her prim cardigan and gabardine slacks.

"I like your jacket," Stephanie Jacob said. They all seemed surprised by Deborah's experiment with grunge, so out of character with her usual preppy peacoat and Talbot's turtlenecks. Perhaps she had decided to exchange tasseled loafers for boots and embrace a new café style chic with leather, the French favorite against the damp chill of December.

"Lord & Taylor," she said. "Phil got it for me on his trip home." Even her Euro-trash look was imported. Elinor felt decidedly drab in her bulky black parka. She felt Deborah examining her with a kind of awed curiosity. It was beyond Deborah's comprehension how a self-respecting woman in her thirties could walk around in vinyl boots, off-brand jeans, such atrocious socks and a black nylon ski coat and pass it off with some sort of flair. Who knew how much time she devoted to seeking out the perfectly tasteful jumper to wear to one of the ladies coffees that they all were mad to attend.

Elinor couldn't be bothered with trying to keep up. And so she didn't. She shopped for herself at the supermarket while she picked up the groceries and was unashamed to wear the plastic boots she found in the women's department of the *Géant Casino*. In Deborah's opinion, she flaunted her apparent bad taste with a kind of enjoyment that was despicable. But Deborah would be returning to the States by the end of the year anyway. Finally, Elinor felt, she would breath a sigh of relief and not worry if Alexi was wearing the same tights she wore yesterday or endure Deborah's ridiculous complaints of being unable to find a respectable pair of shoes after visiting all of the fancy boutiques in Cherbourg. It seemed Deborah would have to move back to the States to find a decent pair of shoes imported from Italy, France or Spain.

"Well, at least someone else is not ashamed to sport a bleach mishap to school," Deborah said, pointing out to Elinor a dime-sized white spot on her navy pullover.

"Thank you, Deborah, I hadn't noticed," Elinor sighed.

"Oh, I do it all the time. All my clothes are ruined. Who can figure out how to do the laundry for a family of four in these teeny washer and dryers? I never knew you could wear a pair of jeans more than once until I moved to France. I mean everyone thinks the French smell because they don't bathe, but the fact is, it's because they don't wash their sweaters. They just need to do a few more loads of laundry." Everyone agreed the American standard of personal hygiene was plainly the highest in the world, and although large portions of the population were lazy and ignorant, the fact that Americans were the nicest smelling culture in the world was no trifle.

"I take everything to the cleaners here. You think I would put one of Phil's one hundred percent pinpoint cotton Brooks Brothers shirts in the laundry?" Deborah gasped.

Suddenly it occurred to Elinor the reason Deborah suffered so much in France. She suddenly pictured her in a state of anxiety, examining the dials on her tiny washer with an arm full of fine washables. It must have nearly driven her mad. That very inconvenience was at the very root of her dislike of this country. How could one live under such conditions? Did she hang them out to dry? Did she iron? She must have been a virtual slave to the laundry, making neat little loads that kept the things running continuously all day. It must have caused her great pain to load all of the Baby Gap pullovers and Gymboree jumpers into that little machine that would grind them up, extorting a whole percentage of the natural fibers from them every time.

They stood together waiting for something else to say. The fact was that they saw each other every day and their lives were very much the same. Certainly they pretended to be productively occupied or made an effort to show up to school wearing sweats and sneakers one day a week to show that they worked out or went to the gym. But really, the trouble was that they all had far too much time on their hands and very little to worry about. Instead their worries were enormous and distant from their immediate lives like global warming and the depletion of the ozone layer, all the garbage and people who didn't recycle. Or wretched children who suffered most particularly at Christmas time, with nothing but sliced turkey loaf, Barbie knock-offs, and the fear that their own children might be tormented by such unfortunate children.

But it seemed they always found each other to stand around with in front of the gate, clustered in an impenetrable fortress of English. Awesome, unscalable walls were constructed around every word they exchanged, every joke they laughed at. Americans are always laughing or making each other laugh, which is not a bad thing in itself. In fact, Elinor was always ready to laugh whenever she could, but laughing excessively puts the French very ill at ease. And in a country where the people were reputed to laugh less than three minutes per day, they can interpret it in no other way than that perhaps *they* are somehow being laughed at. Their American banter and animated gestures separated them entirely from the French women, and Deborah could always be relied upon to say rather loudly, "Great purse, Stephanie!"

"Thanks, I just got it."

"Well, it's great. What is it—a backpack or a shoulder bag?" The purse was removed from Stephanie's shoulder, and she began to demonstrate some of its features and advantages.

"It's both, really. You can wear it as a backpack or on the shoulder. I don't know, for traveling with the kids, I always find that a backpack is great. But for going to the flea market when you're always reaching for your purse, a shoulder bag is terrific."

"Well, the leather is *great*."

Elinor couldn't help wondering if that comment was made for her benefit and was suddenly made aware again of her vinyl boots. What astonished her about Deborah was that although her conversation was dreadfully dull and insupportably artificial, she seemed to hold some unquestioned authority over the conversation. It was these types of conversations that Elinor loathed, and she raised her eyes in boredom and looked up over the group's neatly coiffed heads to catch her, the beautiful Frenchwoman, watching her with interest. Their eyes met long enough for the woman to command her attention and make Elinor acknowledge her in a silent exchange of their similar situations, a hopeful look, perhaps a plea of deliverance, before she turned away to feign attention to what was being said in her own little cluster of elegant French women in lovely scarves and bright berets. What were they talking of, Elinor wanted to know. It was not altogether unlikely that it was about anything very different from what her own group was talking of—a *sac* or *écharpe*, where to find the finest produce, and what ingredient made a truly authentic *petit sale.*

"Elinor, *hello!*" Deborah brought her back into the fortress that she longed to escape. She wanted to know what Elinor was wearing to the Christmas dinner.

"Oh? I have no idea," she said, turning away in her plastic boots.

When the gate opened, the women pushed their way through with their babies and strollers like shopping carts at a clearance sale. Elinor noticed Stephanie Jacob leading her little boy by the hand. He held a Ziploc bag of pretzels clutched in the fist of the other hand.

"No running!" she directed fiercely as he shook free and darted into the crush of women and strollers, tripping and falling cruelly almost immediately. Stephanie snatched him up into her arms to comfort his cries of surprise and embarrassment.

"This horrible black top!" she cried, as if the treacherous French asphalt had tripped her child intentionally.

The courtyard was a small open space in the city, like a window to the sky. Elinor stared at the broken bleak clouds of winter, and for a moment, it seemed they might offer her some escape. Escape from women and babies—she had no patience with a chaotic culture of fervent and fertile females. The French mothers pushed around large healthy babies in sleek buggies and prams, strangled in boiled woolen coats and caps. The baby, leading the whole proud clan home after school, looking bewildered as if he knew he was only entitled to as much happiness as could be rationed among them in a meager apartment in the city. The American women wore the badge of motherhood differently with every accessory money could buy tucked in neat little compartments of their more high-tech, streamlined strollers. And Stephanie Jacob was ready to hand out a Band-Aid, Babywipe, juice box or pretzel stick at your child's slightest whimper. Elinor watched the women returning casserole dishes from dinner parties and swapping video tapes in the frenzied exchange of a bazaar or crowded market. Deborah Knolls charged toward her with her tidy children in tow.

"See ya Saturday."

Elinor waved and made for her own children, who she saw emerge from the bedlam.

"Mommy! Mommy! Look what I made!" Alexi was holding an adorably wrapped package in homemade Christmas paper, fumbling at it with her fingers to open it and show her. She could hardly suppress her joy. "Open it Mommy! Open it!" Little Clara had a little package, too, something they had made at school as Christmas presents. Elinor looked at them both and slowly stopped Alexi's fingers from the ribbon. "No, sweetie, we'll open it at home."

Elinor wished to get off the playground. She was a selfish creature, she scolded herself, but she couldn't forget the woman's interested look. What was in that look—that electrically charged look that made the world stand still? Gazing silently at the happy little faces of her girls, she was reminded of what a fool she was to have allowed herself to become so susceptible to someone she didn't even know. What was this? Nothing. And certainly nothing important. It was simply an idea, a longing, and a desire to understand the French. Something she had made up. This love affair with France, with *her*, all existed in her head. To be infatuated with another woman's beauty, a stranger, when standing before her was the flesh of her flesh, begging her to notice them and enjoy their offerings at least as much as they did, made her thoroughly ashamed of herself.

She took Alexi's little hand in hers and lifted Clara up to make her escape, and they walked out into the street. Elinor said nothing, feeling embarrassed and distracted, looking straight ahead as she moved down the sidewalk toward the car.

"Here, *looook!*" Alexi squealed. Elinor turned to see Alexi holding a little glass yogurt jar, decorated with bits of colored tissue paper and a candle in it in her outstretched hand. It was truly pretty. The pretty wrapping paper was torn and wadded up in her other little fist. She pulled the child to her with tears in her eyes, "Alexi, it's beautiful," she whispered. "It's the most beautiful thing I've ever seen."

Alexi beamed with a kind of wide-eyed wonder and disbelief that the small offering was indeed precious and could bring her as much joy as it did her. Clara's was to be opened, too, and she gushed over it as well, but Elinor knew little Clara was so certain of her devotion and of her own irresistibility that there was no question her mommy must love her lovely little twig picture frame with a picture of herself making it in class. Clara received Elinor's kiss with quiet satisfaction, while Alexi demanded reassurance every block or so on the ride home from school. "Isn't it pretty Mommy?"

7

Saturday morning Elinor ran into Stephanie Jacob and her husband at the flea market. Elinor was carrying another painted statue of Christ under her arm for her collection. She had paid five hundred francs, about seventy-five dollars, for him. He was so beautiful, he was almost frightening. His ancient face was nearly black with age, the paint polished smooth by the heavy dank air of the church where he had certainly stood for more than a century. Elinor was walking by. She loved the flea market. Her house was a veritable odd museum of strange objects she had found at the flea market, and she had made herself a marvelous religious art collection of painted saints, silently watching her in a heap on her bed, crying over the woman from the school or listening to the awful things she might shout at the children or her husband. She would catch their serene expression over the heads of her family and stop for a moment to meet their solemn gaze. They never seemed to pass judgment or scold her for her preposterous passions, but were always present and bemused.

It was Brad Jacob who stopped her. They had been standing at a booth of an expensive looking dealer of what looked like mostly *faience*.

"Hey, Elinor, how much would you offer for something like that?" he asked. He was pointing to some ostentatious looking vase or something mounted on bronze claws. The first thing that popped into her head was, nothing. She wouldn't offer anything. The price was marked five thousand francs, the price of a modest armoire in France.

"Well, I don't know," she hesitated, "I don't really know that much about porcelain."

"He says it's a hundred years old," he said excitedly.

"I don't know. He can tell you anything he wants," she said. She was trying to be helpful. "I don't really recognize the style."

"Well, how much would you offer him?" he persisted.

She never usually spent over a hundred dollars or so at the flea market, a place to pick up a *petite lampe*, a tea cup, an obscure painting or funky mirror.

"Don't ask me this," she begged. She did not wish to give them advice. The idea seemed wrought with consequence. Perhaps it was his position, although she thought that didn't bother her. It was more his own notion of his position that made her uncomfortable. He stood staring at her, waiting, almost pleadingly, and Elinor thought, what did he want? What did she know? With her wacky religious icons, she knew nothing of antiques. They seemed to be always studying her with questions, as if they might discover through something that she might say, that she was a witch, or a lesbian for having a rather large copy of the *Birth of Venus* hanging in her living room—or perhaps lately, she had reason to be paranoid.

Stephanie regarded her with curiosity that seemed to brighten for a moment, delighting in the excitement of talking rather causally without revealing her prejudice or suspicion of someone so unconventional. She was staring, rather alarmed, at the statue Elinor had under her arm.

"I don't know . . . fifteen hundred," Elinor said, giving up.

"Good!" he exclaimed. "I offered three thousand for both of them," and he pointed to another thing in the same pattern standing on bronze claws. What are you going to do with *that*, Elinor wondered.

"Well, that sounds about right," she assured him. She felt sorry for them, for the superiority they felt over her, a person who collected statues of the Virgin Mary and Christ for their beauty in some blasphemous way, like Madonna wearing crucifixes in the eighties. Elinor threatened what they considered to be proper churchgoing values that emanated from their well-bred perch that sat on their corner of Rue Saint Exupery. Elinor felt sorry for her, freezing in the enormous apartments of her house alone after she dropped the children off at school, amongst her tasteful furniture and her attempts to make the high baroque ceilings and cold tile floors as cozy as the bonus room back in the States where they had proper ties to the community, going to church with their family, though never feeling any particular connection with any of the rest of the unfortunate people who populated the planet. Stephanie Jacob was certain she had nothing in common with the rest of lurid humanity that surrounded her, and she organized a Bible study group at her home, as exclusive and fanatic as any dead poet's society, to suffer her situation rather than enjoy it in a way in which Elinor wasn't at all sure Jesus would approve. Certainly without his permission, Jesus was her silent confirmation that what she did and how she behaved, with her nose wrinkled up in distaste, was quite right and correct.

"What did you find?" Stephanie asked, although it was unmistakable.

"Jesus," Elinor said, "I found Jesus." Elinor held up the statue, kind of in her face, as if it might scare her. "I collect these," she said as an explanation. "You can find them all over the place here. I never pay much. They have been discarded along with the religion they represent as so *unraisonable*," she laughed. "Isn't he beautiful?"

"Yes," Stephanie said, although Elinor knew she didn't mean it. "They're so into idolatry here."

At first, Elinor almost ignored her, but Stephanie interested her, and she was curious.

"What do you mean?" Elinor asked.

"The Catholics, I mean, they're into idolatry," she whispered, as if anyone might be paying any attention at all to their conversation in English. Elinor knew she must tread lightly here so as to not injure such precious opinions. Opinions like these, although worn vulnerably upon their sleeves, in no way contribute to insecurity as any other quirks or idiosyncrasies might, however tender the spots might be that they protect. These opinions are nursed and fed like cavalry ready to be launched into attack at the slightest hair raised in opposition. It is useless to persuade the narrow-minded to open up. They enjoy their condition far too much to let a cold draft under the cozy covers. They prefer to pull the blankets up over their heads and despise the world, blaming everyone bad for their own isolation in it. Religion is usually the last wicked spell of control they can conjure up, as mystical and powerful as witchcraft and sorcery and as effective as any curse.

Elinor glanced at Stephanie's husband to see if he would betray how she made him suffer.

"No, I don't think they are," Elinor said. It was clear Stephanie Jacob understood nothing of the world, had never been moved by beauty or the passion to express it herself and had a heart so chipped at and chiseled away by all her disappointments and then reshaped with propriety and convention that she mistook for salvation. "I just think they're very expressive and they have left wonderful cathedrals and monuments to their faith. Their religion has civilized the Western world, and if they're going to sell their art at the flea market for three hundred francs, I'm happy to pay," Elinor said, feeling suddenly terribly sad. It seemed a shame to live in a free world, so stifled by convention. The fact was that she was sick of having her new independence trespassed upon so frequently by the other expatriates in town.

That afternoon, Victor and the girls went out shopping and left her alone to feel the foolishness of her behavior and to see and understand her distorted viewpoint. She wandered lethargically through the house, drifting into rooms to find snail shells, sand, pebbles from the vineyard, twigs tied together with string, scissors, a little heap of muddy boots, a little puddle of pee-pee on the bathroom floor, one of mommy's scarves tied in knots, and a plastic sand pail, tiny tea cups and saucers. She picked up the odd little collection and put it in the pail and swept up the dirt with sudden irritation. Would they never learn to take off their boots outside? Then she went into the kitchen to clear away the lunch dishes.

It is naturally ridiculous that women should be in love with each other, but it is no less unlikely. Their very natures are competitive and vain. Women are either critical of their own appearance or obsessed with it. A woman must be beautiful or she has failed somehow to meet the expectations of her very purpose. All her inadequacies may be the result of her lack of beauty. If she is to accomplish great things, it may be in spite of her good looks or to spite her plain looks. Beautiful women need not be clever, because they don't have to be and are never expected to be. They don't even have to be particularly interesting, as Elinor feared might be the case with the beautiful French woman. And it is always fascinating to discover when a beautiful woman is intelligent, not that it matters much, but one always feels compelled to add, "and she's clever, too." And then we are to all draw back in surprise and alarm and declare, "Amazing! Why, it doesn't seem fair!" That's the reason love or attraction between two women is impossible, she decided, especially between two French women. Because they are themselves so elegant. The art of being seductive is so practiced in this country and the stakes are so high. Not to mention the competition is brutal. That's why in France, mothers name their girls Latitia and in the States they name their girls sensible names like Carolyn. Because the French mother wishes her daughter to be a graceful and elegant young lady or a least an anorexic model. And American mothers wish their daughters to go to Stanford and kick ass and take names in the way she wishes she had done. This very difference bands American women together in camaraderie and sets French women against each other in competition. Women do not fall in love with other beautiful women. It is absurd. They hate each other, although there is no woman who is extraordinary herself who does not admire extraordinary qualities in other women. But she had been distracted from her family and children too long with this preoccupation, she decided. I am humiliating my children in the pursuit of this, Elinor thought, and wished, longed for something that would soften her heart to her beautiful little

Alexi when she seemed to always be on the receiving end of her frustration and disgust with herself for being such a miserable mother.

Victor and the girls brought home a beautiful Christmas tree, and Elinor took out the Christmas decorations from the garage. She began to relax and enjoy her children decorating the tree, although it somehow seemed more stressful than it should be. Victor urged her to take a glass of port and some stollen to put her more at ease. She shook her head.

"What's the matter? You don't love me," he said miserably as if he understood her distraction. And when she looked into his large brown eyes, she thought, of course, she loved him. He was everything capable and good. In fact she loved him more than ever, she thought, with his thick wool turtleneck and unshaven face, bringing home a Christmas tree for them to decorate.

She slid her arms around his waist. "I love you . . . as much as I can," she said, grinning to make him laugh. He believed she could make him happy and was always astonished and disappointed when she didn't. She stood in his arms, and he held her tight, remarkably tight, so that she felt suddenly that she couldn't breathe.

"I'm so rich," he said. "I'm so lucky to have you and the girls." He buried his face in her neck and she thought, this is where I belong. This is what happiness is—to be so loved and taken care of.

He wanted to videotape. That made her even more uneasy, and she took the glass of port and drained it. She was terrified that her distraction might be evident or apparent on tape.

Alexi loved going through all the ornaments that she remembered from the years past, particularly the ones Elinor had let her pick out each year on their trips to Alsace. Alexi had a wonderful artistic sense of the world, entirely colored by her brilliant imagination. In her world, strange and marvelous things happened, and one could never be sure if what she said was true, had indeed happened, not because she was lying, but because that was indeed how it had happened for her—how she had experienced whatever it was. She was fascinated by flowers, insects, snails and other creatures of nature. She drew them in the most fantastic Dr. Seuss interpretations of whatever she saw and put them in picture frames she made from shoe boxes. Elinor was always proud of her creations— they were truly wonderful.

Alexi dug around in the boxes of the fragile ornaments, and Elinor scolded her—"Be careful, slow down, be patient." She was always trying to contain Alexi's marvelous enthusiasm. Happily, the child never listened to her anyway. She certainly marched to the beat of her own band, springing from bed in the morning and running into their room to wake them up and say good morning.

"Mommy, I'm done!" she would say, meaning sleeping. "Do we have school this morning?" she always asked on Saturday, knowing the delightful answer already, but waiting to hear Elinor say it so she could savor the idea.

"No," Elinor would groan. Alexi couldn't sleep past the crack of dawn especially on Saturday, and although Elinor wished she could meet her enthusiasm even if she didn't have to wake up and get her ready for school, she would tell her, "You can go down and color or watch cartoons," and would roll over and go back to sleep until Clara woke up.

When Alexi was on a mission, nothing could stop her. She was looking for something specific she wanted to put on the tree, opening the tissue paper that protected the other delicate ornaments Elinor had inherited from her mother or the ones she and Victor had received at their wedding. But the reality was, Elinor was exhausted. The children often exhausted her. The nature of her life and her position of responsibility in it made her stand at the kitchen counter inundated with the awesome responsibility of raising daughters. So she ignored the argument that was escalating over who would spread the Nutella on the bread. She found herself simply walking away. She would let them sort out such a trivial dispute for themselves. Perhaps it was her fault they were behaving like such little beasts, trapped in the house while it sleeted outside. Certainly it was her lack of attention, love and poring over their needs as she watched her American girlfriends do with their own children. Perhaps she must stop despising them all for raising such self-centered bourgeois little creatures and indulge her own children a bit more at least with her attention. After all, all you need to succeed and be happy in life was a healthy dose of self-esteem and short-term memory. What was the good of protecting your children from the hundreds of distractions the average child consumed daily when they just seemed to suffer from the deprivation.

She was busy helping little Clara put an ornament she had chosen onto the tree when she heard the shattering of glass on the hard tile floor of the house. Alexi looked up, surprised and horrified. She had found the precious little blown-glass reindeer she had been searching for. She had picked it out in Murano last year, and Elinor had praised her for having found the most beautiful ornament. Indeed it was beautiful and she had been so proud of herself to be the one to find it and pick it out from among all the others. Then the tears broke.

"I broke it Mommy!" she cried. "I dropped it! I'm not careful!" she wailed in anguish. "I broke the most beautiful ornament!" Elinor picked her up and held her head close to her cheek. "It's okay. Mommy's not mad," she tried to say, but Alexi would not be comforted. "I broke my reindeer," she said with such catastrophic prophetic self-knowledge, as if she would forsake the things she loved her whole life. Elinor held her tight and whispered in her ear, "It was an accident, you didn't mean to." After several moments, Alexi's grip loosened, and she let go and tried to carry on with the decorating, but even the decorating, something she loved, like making something or putting up a picture she had drawn in her room, could not console the loss of the little glass ornament, and her spirits could not be lifted.

It was the evening of the Annual International Women's Association Christmas dinner where the international community all turned out like movie stars in glamorous evening dress—the women in wraps and tiny purses, the men leading them in, holding hands, expectant, as if they were on a date. By the time the babysitter Veronique arrived, Alexi was quite tired and sullen, but happy as usual with the idea of Veronique, the pretty babysitter, and took her hand to show her the tree. Elinor told Veronique to give them some cake, read them a story and put them to bed before nine. She always let them stay up a bit longer than usual when she and Victor went out. Then Elinor went up to dress. When she was finished, checked herself in the mirror in her red satin blouse, earrings that Victor had given her, and a narrow black skirt, and she thought she must look far too glamorous—vampy even to the conservative families she would dine with that evening—to be a very good mother who must care a great deal more for parties and dinners than for staying at home naturally with her children.

When they arrived at dinner, everyone was in their best clothes and had certainly all taken a shower or shaved before coming. There was much concern and going on about where to sit, at what table and with whom to sit. It was all very silly how adults behaved in quite the same manner in which they did as adolescents in high school. Elinor and Karen decided to sit together, behaving like teenagers as well, taking each other by the arm as they walked into the dining room.

She was being waved down by Stephanie Jacob and her husband who were already at a table when she walked in. Mrs. Jacob was trying to get Elinor's attention to sit with them, because her table was not filling up very quickly, and that was never a good thing. Elinor didn't think Mrs. Jacob could possibly truly like her, or even want to spend the evening in her company, but perhaps there was really no one else at the gathering worth the Jacobs' notice anyway.

Stephanie Jacob and her husband were convinced that France was nothing at all like what they were expecting, and from the very beginning, she occupied herself in sizing up all the inadequacies of her new situation. He was a top executive brought over in finance and clearly fancied himself important enough to rent her an enormous baroque mansion that occupied an entire city block, not knowing that the demonstration or presumption of wealth in France is never as impressive or even important as it is in the States.

"It doesn't seem that big when you're inside," she insisted after sensing the ostentation of it and visiting many of the other expatriate families in their moderate accommodations and considering the Durtols themselves occupied a modest apartment in the city. Stephanie worried, as was her habit, what people might think. When the gloom of winter settled into the city, she began to see it as a great disadvantage not only to their comfort and pocketbook, but she began to respond uncomfortably to people who questioned her curiously about how she was settling in.

"Well, we really don't have any neighbors, I mean, we have neighbors but . . . well, we haven't really gotten to know any of them yet," she said, eager to demonstrate the house's disadvantages rather than to appear as if she were gloating or that she might enjoy such an extravagance. This was not at all the impression she wanted to make or the opinion she held of herself. She was humility itself. Everything in her attitude and appearance spoke of her quiet unpretentiousness.

She didn't have neighbors, of course, because she was taking up the entire city block and the French are very cautious and certainly openly suspicious of Americans moving into one of their historical landmarks. They could not know how modest and what a good Christian she was which must always be acceptable, even to a confused culture of people who worshiped Mary.

Although Mr. Jacob enjoyed setting himself apart well enough, she did not. She rather tolerated his need for worldly possessions. Her needs were simple and were mostly fulfilled and validated by her church at home, far away where it could no longer offer her the comfort she needed in the face of a hostile world.

She always looked as if she were in pain. As if her life were a series of brutal encounters with a vulgar culture of people less fortunate, more ignorant, and morally inferior to her well brought up manners and correct values. She always kept a good Christian place for them in her heart, simply by pitying them, with as much sympathy as she treated everyone with whom she felt no associations with their failings. Hers was a singular existence, and nothing could move her compassion more than the tender tears of her own aristocratic children as she peeled them off of herself each morning, sending them off to school to suffer the discomfort and the severity of the French school. She was trying to get Elinor's attention, and Elinor couldn't ignore her and not sit with them without being rude.

Elinor approached their table reluctantly and greeted them politely.

"I hope you will join us," Brad Jacob said directly to her as if she should understand she were being paid a special compliment with his attention.

"By all means," she said, knowing that this could only be interesting. "This is my husband, Victor."

Brad Jacob took Victor's working class hand in his aristocratic one and shook it patronizingly. He was big and blond and handsome. Stephanie paled in comparison to her handsome husband whose confidence was equal to his ambition. There was a hint in her appearance that she had once been very pretty, but any looks that she might have once claimed for herself, were overshadowed by the presence of her shining husband and had been worn away with worry. She was dressed gaily in a long black velvet skirt and a red herringbone jacket, but Elinor knew she was miserable, knew that she was disappointing to her husband. He seemed convinced he deserved more, and the only thing that civilizes a man is the wish to please his wife. And what would become of her when this wish was gone?

Stephanie Jacob was not at all ready to make the best of her situation. Rather, she seemed quite determined to make the worst of it. Most of all, Elinor felt her cold stare of disapproval.

"How did you make out at the flea market?" Elinor asked presently. "Did you find anything?"

"Yes, the vases," Stephanie said with a defeated sigh, bringing her eyebrows together in pain and concern.

"Well, good," Elinor said, confused by her evident discontent.

Stephanie leaned over and whispered, "I think we got taken."

"Oh?"

Mrs. Jacob had spent the rest of the day being disappointed and angry, she explained, after having discovered a bar code stuck to the bottom of one of the vases. Clearly it was not a hundred years old after all. She made Elinor promise not to say anything—her husband still didn't know.

"I'm afraid it might upset him," she said, looking worried. She vowed never to visit the flea market again and could never again be persuaded to buy something from one of the ill-reputed merchants. Her bitterness was surprising, and Elinor could not help but feel that a great vanity was concealed in her humility. What Mrs. Jacob wished to pass off as goodness and concern was an inclination to find fault. She insisted she could not understand why they hadn't served the aperitifs in the lounge and were attempting to do so in the dining room where one was forced to be confined to the group at their table. It seemed the fault of the British ladies who had placed themselves in charge of the gathering.

"I feel like we're at the British ladies convention," she sneered, as if a sneer could be accompanied by a pained look of sympathy so no one could mistake her good intentions.

The Jacobs both looked a little squeamish when the food arrived. Elinor watched Stephanie poke at the little squid tentacles suspiciously with her fork, delicately moving them aside to see if she could find something in the sauce of her seafood *feuillete* that was more familiar and less horrifying.

At the other end of the table sat Frank and Patricia Parker. Frank was very handsome and equally boring. Patricia was plain with a great deal of unchecked enthusiasm and no ability to contain or stop herself from saying or doing whatever silly thing popped into her head. They reminded Elinor of Burt and Ernie on *Sesame Street*. Frank, serious and annoyed, even looked strikingly like Burt. And Patricia had all of Ernie's good-natured goofiness. They seemed so ill-suited for one another that she imagined them to have two separate twin beds in the room they shared with the initials E and B monogrammed on the headboards.

Elinor knew the handsome Frank wanted to sleep with her, even though there had never been more than ten words spoken between them. He imagined he deserved better, but was unfortunately shackled with an unstylish wife who adored him. At family dinner gatherings, or one of Deborah's cocktail parties, Elinor would catch him staring at her, silently studying her and always attempting to engage her in conversation. They would usually talk of travel, where he had visited, and the wine tasting tours he had taken. The conversation could never be anything but boring along these lines, or pick up any kind of speed or direction, the shallowness of his ideas, and his lack of interest in anything other than perhaps how good he looked in the turtleneck he was wearing prevented them from ever having anything to say.

She remembered one evening at Deborah's, they had both come alone. Patricia, although married to Frank, spent very little time actually living with him in France and was constantly in the States visiting her mother, and Victor was away in Finland working. Frank kept eyeing her all night with some kind of secret satisfaction in the notion that because their spouses were both out of town, they must certainly end up together.

Finally, standing in a group with him, she could see his anticipation and eager attempts to converse.

"Where's Victor?" he finally dared.

"He's in Finland working. And Patricia, I see is out of town as well?"

"Yes," he said, "she's visiting her mother." He could hardly disguise his enthusiasm.

"Well, since we're both single here tonight, and you're such an exceptionally handsome fellow, we ought to just get a cab and go home together," she surprised him by saying.

She watched him squirm for a reply that would meet that right on with intelligence and candor, but his wit was out of practice. It really had never been exercised, and it was loath to begin now. Although his head was held up upon his thick neck and broad shoulders, he had never really needed to be clever, and if there had been any spark of originality before, let's say in college, it had been neatly swept up and out of sight under the carpet with all his other offending ideas when he had married Patricia. But now, while everyone waited for him to be clever, all he could do was take another sip of his drink and smile sheepishly, instantly regretting his attraction to her—that she should size up his fancy so accurately, making him feel silly and girlish. He sensed he was being made fun of. In his own bland life he had learned to ignore his passions. Pack them up into little boxes and bury them in the basement under the Christmas decorations.

And now, he sat sulkily at the end of the table refusing to look at Elinor. She watched him watching his wife as if she were some volatile child whose behavior or something that she would say in childish innocence might embarrass the whole room. He almost seemed prepared to duck a flying mushroom or pearl onion she might fling at him from her plate, laughing, "Stop it, silly!"

"Elinor, your children speak very good French, they even sound

French. Do you speak to them at home in French?" Stephanie could hardly suppress her curiosity in Victor. He was dark and foreign with a decidedly old-world formality in his manner that she determined was arrogant and exclusive and would hazard nothing with the kind of gaiety and openness that would satisfy her. He had an accent. Was he French? She was burning to know.

"Oh, I know," said Patricia Parker, insisting she have her share in the conversation. She was, after all, an old hand, too, having lived at least two years in France herself. "After living here for two years, Stephanie, your kids will speak perfect French, too. My kids do. You should hear our Jonathan's accent. It's amazing. It's perfect. All his teachers tell him it's the perfect French accent. You should hear him say *Mercredi*. Get him to say *Mercredi*. You have to get him to say *Mercredi!*"

Stephanie was undaunted in her pursuit of what it was specifically that placed Elinor in her unusual category that she suspected might be objectionable. Certainly being married to a foreigner had something to do with it.

"So where did you two meet?" she continued curiously to Victor.

"At graduate school. I came to the States from Romania," he said to relieve her efforts.

Stephanie colored slightly, and then said suddenly, "That's funny, because in the book I'm reading the Antichrist is a Romanian named Carpathia."

"Oh?" Elinor said. "Fancy that, Victor, the Antichrist is Romanian. That *is* funny. And what book is that?"

"*Left Behind*," Stephanie said.

Elinor thought she must be joking.

"Heaven by this account happens to look very like suburban America, as secure as a subdivision named Fervent Meadows with as many amenities and a members-only clubhouse for Christians, golf games with Jesus, and an Olympic-sized baptismal pool." She thought her comment would be hilarious. Instead it inspired a horrified silence. Brad Jacob looked amazed and then embarrassed. He began to tell of a dreadful dinner party he had been forced to attend in the States while he was home on business.

"The plate of food was enormous and was wolfed down in half an hour, and the conversation was mostly about their stuff, investments and sports. Which is really tedious, you know. I believe you're right," he directed to Elinor, "Americans do seem to look for their salvation in material things," he finished majestically.

"And you don't?" Elinor said as innocently as possible and then daintily placed a forkful of *truffade* in her mouth. Brad Jacob was truly surprised by the fact that she seemed to make no consideration for who he was. This being such a rare occurrence in his experience, he was both indignant and delighted. He didn't really know what to do, so he smiled.

"I have material things as everybody does, but I don't seek my salvation in them. And I certainly don't make them the topic of conversation at a dinner party."

"Really? What *do* you make your conversation at a dinner party?" she said with anticipation.

He took a moment to consider and then said, "Did you know that in the entrance to the paleontology museum at the Jardin des Plantes is a statue of a guy named Lamarck who they call 'The Father of Evolution' in giant letters! And that in the Luxembourg Gardens there is a guy named Branly whose pedestal proclaims him to be the father of wireless communication, radiotelegraph and television?"

"How absurd and presumptuous," Elinor said, smiling. "I agree with you that there's very little good conversation anymore which involves the open expression of opinions. People today *expect* to disagree with each other and because of this, take very little pleasure in each other's company. It is inevitable that dinner parties are pleasant only for what is being served at the table."

"Or are as interesting as the people who sit around the table," he said enjoying himself immensely. Elinor could feel Stephanie getting uncomfortable, inevitably becoming jealous of her husband's attention. Husbands—as if Elinor would want anyone else's when she'd already got one of her own. It was absurd.

Brad Jacob began to say how frightfully barbaric it is to carry one's Christmas turkey home in a cage and added that he could find no other alternative here in France. Finishing off her petit café that she had watched them both refuse at the end of the dreadful meal, Elinor assured him that this year they had decided to spare themselves the discomfort and nasty business of preparing such fresh poultry by going home to spend Christmas at her mother's.

8

When school started again in January, Elinor assured herself she had completely forgotten Elisabeth's mommy and was determined to disregard her at all cost, but as she led her girls up to the school gate on the Monday after the Christmas holiday, they ran head-on into each other as the woman was coming out from having already dropped off her children. They both acknowledged each other with an awkward "bonjour." It seemed unavoidable, and Elinor was startled by how beautiful she looked, her fine strong features enhanced with makeup. The woman had her hair down, and it shone in the sunshine of the morning. She was wearing a bright sweater under her open coat which accentuated her lovely form beneath. Where was she going looking so good? Her life could not be so unlike hers, Elinor thought, and began to suspect the woman must be crazy, as women often were who stayed at home with the children. Elinor even thought she might forgive her. It was true how absolutely un-French her behavior must have been. Perhaps it was naturally understandable that the woman might have mistook her meaning.

Elinor had used *tu* instead of *vous,* assuming an inappropriate familiarity that never existed between them. Although the formality of it annoyed her, Elinor understood the necessity of maintaining distance between people. The French are never so eager to form new friendships as Americans are and are in fact quite suspicious of their ridiculous gregariousness. They recognize a vague anxiety in the understanding that venturing to form new friendships is not without obligation, particularly in communities, such as the school, where one's narrow privacy could so easily be trespassed upon, regularly even. Certainly she wished to preserve a distance that did not exist in the actual proximity of their lives. It was true, the usual daily routine could so easily be upset by the intrusion of others, by the obligation of an uncomfortable friendliness which is very awkward for them and they prefer to avoid at all cost—feeling awkward or placing themselves in situations that present the possibility of feeling awkward. Americans have an oblivious self-assurance and spontaneity that inspires apprehension in the French. They feel tremendous pressure in conversation to know "what to say." They must be witty, intelligent, and the worst error is to be cliché, synonymous with boring—say nothing rather than be tiresome.

Elinor had gathered in her observation of the woman that she must live quite near the school. What had made her make such an effort to present herself so well at school at eight in the morning to drop the children off? Elinor resolved that she could do nothing but dislike her even more for looking so great, although the woman began to show in her manner an open and direct interest. There was in her greeting today a certain understanding, an acceptance of some connection or rapport that existed between them. And when the woman gave her a bashful grin, Elinor suddenly knew in her address, that she had made the effort with her appearance in the anticipation of meeting *her.* Her look was vaguely come-hither, coquettish even, so that Elinor was suddenly furious that the woman should flirt with her so confidently as if Elinor were a masculine admirer or suitor. And all this she coveyed in a look and a gesture that Elinor could not mistake because she had practiced it herself with men.

❧

That afternoon while Elinor waited in the courtyard to collect the children at school, she saw the Frenchwoman's apparent husband with the twins, waiting for their two older girls. She knew it must be him and was momentarily struck and could not help staring. Her observation of Frenchmen was almost always disappointing—they were unfortunately small, and often ill-groomed. They generally lacked the masculinity and gallantry of the more well-built, large, and good-natured American men that she was so familiar with. Elinor did not imagine the woman's husband could be anything different than what could invariably be put into two categories—unattractive, small, and fervent family men with occupations or undesirable disreputable looking men unable to shake their adolescence or secure adequate employment, who in their thirties often clad themselves in worn leather jackets, were habitually unshaven, and who she often noticed at the supermarket in the middle of the day pushing the shopping cart around with a rather misfortunate looking child in the front, allowing their wives to bring home an inadequate income.

However, he was tall, handsome, and very obviously serious. He looked like some wild poet or romantic hero from a novel with pale eyes and unruly blond hair. His features were hawk-like. His large blue eyes, set wide apart on each side of his aquiline nose, gave him a magnificent profile. He was almost more remarkable than his wife. Elinor couldn't help staring and then looked into Elisabeth's and Antoine's faces to see traces of him in them. Clearly it was from him that Elisabeth had inherited her fair hair and pale skin. He was lovely and elegant, not large or coarse. He could have been Lord Byron or a fair Heathcliff in *Wuthering Heights*. Elinor stared, she knew she did. He noticed her staring and gave her an arrogant grin. She peered into his pale eyes and wanted to know what he was thinking. His good looks and evident solemnity frightened her. And although she couldn't help staring, she was sure her evident interest in him would confirm her infatuation with his wife. She was startled and ashamed into recognizing the absurdity of her own longing. The woman was married and had his beautiful children. She was married to Victor and had his beautiful children—Victor who was handsome and tolerant, who she had picked largely for his beauty. Her own interest might have turned to jealousy if they became friends and Victor might meet her, see her, recognize something Elinor was sure was even more desirable about her than mere beauty—her cool self-confidence, aloof sensuality, and proud composure. Love between women is a delicate thing, the slightest jealously might upset it. She turned away from him to walk out of the courtyard with her children to avoid a curious approach that she may have encouraged with her interest.

9

The months of the school year passed and Grace Elton arrived—her name was Grace. She had such a tidy, unexceptional but pretty appearance, it depressed Elinor. She had some accessible, simple allure that raised no questions or argument—some sex appeal in the very ordinary quality of her beauty. Something people refer to as girl-next-door good looks and unremarkable style, wearing stretch pants and high heels. She widened at the hips and then tapered precariously on her tasteful stilettos.

Deborah Knolls had bought a new Louis Philippe armoire and *biblioteque* and had a coffee at her house for everyone to welcome Grace and admire her furniture. Deborah's house was impeccably decorated, with tasteful furnishings that were perfectly representative of her and her husband's ambitions in life. Nothing in the house raised any question or controversy as to who they were. She had achieved the perfect harmony between family pieces she had inherited and tasteful pieces she and her husband had acquired together. They, so well matched for one another, were clearly of one mind—"nothing too ornate or decadent, we prefer the simplicity of Louis Philippe"—to something more vulgar, she meant, like the morally debauched Louis. The walls were hung with large wedding portraits like great masterpieces of art—a monument to the value she placed on domestic felicity in marriage and family as well as to the most important day of her life. And her wedding china was as perfectly displayed in a Colonial American china cabinet as it had been in the department store from which she had chosen the pattern.

Elinor heard Deborah entertaining the company in the kitchen while she made what she announced to everyone's delight Dunkin' Donuts coffee that she had brought back from the States. She had been home for the holidays. The French coffee was much too strong as was the culture that often shocked with its frank enjoyment of pungent flavors, odors, tastes and manners.

"Now *I*," Grace Elton began, immediately drawing the group's attention, "have never had trouble making a good cup of coffee. I use Maxwell House individual pods. They're designed to make a perfect cup of coffee every time by combining the perfect coffee-to-water ratio that I have discovered. You just throw the little packet into your Home Café and *presto*—great coffee." Everyone stared at her, baffled. "Perhaps you haven't heard of them, or maybe they came out after you all left. But they're *sooo* easy! I'm sure they must have them here in France?" Someone said no, they didn't think so.

"Well, everybody uses them in the States. In fact, one of my girlfriends from Wellesley is sending me some." Grace had let everyone know at her earliest convenience that she had somehow miraculously gone to Wellesley and because of her brilliance, had stepped out of her own culture of the South where she was raised and had catapulted herself into the distinguished alumnae of the Ivy League with all its obvious advantages. She had worked in New York after college and began to say on what particular block was her office. It was in Lower Manhattan, just a few blocks, *enormous blocks*, because in New York, the city blocks were enormous—they were huge, very long blocks indeed, from Wall Street.

"Really?" Deborah said, "I thought a city block was pretty much a city block?"

"No, I fancy not. Not in Lower Manhattan," Grace continued, telling how she used to eat at this "*darling* deli on Second Ave."

Grace's manners seemed to unite an eagerness to please with a self-satisfaction that inspired immediate confusion and indignation in the group. She boasted of her perfect planning and preparation for their move to France. She had come fully prepared to face the inconveniences and deficiencies of France and had arranged a condensed-soup connection in the States before her departure. "I simply can't cook anything without them," she said. She had even come prepared with a Berlitz course as a quick review. She had studied two years of French at Wellesley already and had excellent comprehension and pronunciation, her instructor had told her, and she was poised to collide with the French culture at the earliest *opportunité*.

These women were not tourists on holiday in France, enjoying themselves. Living in France was entirely another matter. It required adapting oneself to conditions quite beneath what they were accustomed to. Their lives were cumbersome and inconvenient, made more unbearable by being surrounded by people who insisted on conducting themselves in French as if it were the most natural and easy thing to do.

Deborah tried to give her some advice on navigating the airport because Grace was shocked by the apparent absence of clearly marked wings, halls, color-coded terminals and gates and was furious with the lack of effort and vague directions she received from the airport personnel. In fact, there didn't seem to be any specified personnel or staff at the ludicrous airport at all. And if you were occasionally lucky enough to find someone in a uniform or who worked for the airlines, for example, they would certainly be of no help at all or they were on their way to smoke a cigarette or get a coffee and had no interest in properly directing American tourists come to invade their national treasure—Paris. French people were horribly rude and inefficient.

It was true. Elinor remembered dragging Alexi round about the place, seemingly designed by some existential French playwright seeking to create irony and comedy in the kind of entrances and slamming of doors of a French farce, turning down dubious corridors or tunnels looking for a toilet. In the States, there's always a restroom with about sixty stalls every fifty meters or so. But in Charles de Gaulle, after hunting furiously for a full half an hour and getting misdirected several times, she finally found one with two stalls and a sink. Behind the two half-size swinging doors at the entrance was a flight attendant changing her panty hose in the narrow space between the stalls and the sink. As Elinor entered, a woman standing near the wall accosted her for money, and she explained that it was only Alexi who would be using the toilet, but the woman insisted they both pay. Elinor gave her 20 francs and helped Alexi to use the potty.

Deborah said that the way she was able to deal with them was to refuse to speak French. "Just announce very loudly, WHERE'S THE TOILET? or WHAT GATE IS THIS? And if that doesn't work, just threaten to have your child pee on the floor right in front of them."

Everyone laughed. Deborah definitely knew how to take the bull by the horns. Elinor admired her for that.

"Well, my French is good enough, and I always find that the French are often even more helpful if you at least make an effort. You will never regret speaking to them in their own language, and I always find it interesting to discover new people and places. It makes life an adventure, you know. And I've been told that my French is as good as someone who's lived here two years at least."

Deborah hated Grace for saying this, and the subject was changed to Harry Potter and the movies that were made from the books.

"We don't allow those books for the kids," Stephanie Jacob expressed with a decided wariness in her voice.

"Why?" Deborah said with curiosity.

"Well, there have been questions raised in the Christian community about some of the content."

"What content?" Deborah asked a little surprised.

"Well, they're really very dark and about magic and sorcery."

Stephanie said it with her pained look, as if her concern was kindly meant to inform. Elinor could sense a bit of tension developing in the direction of the conversation that she always found uncomfortable between friends who might not share the same opinions yet are naturally hesitant to defend themselves when they feel no need to be defensive and persons who think their opinions are so right and correct they should be announced in polite conversation and adopted by everyone. Elinor also hated this sort of debate, that something as harmless as *Harry Potter*, a book that had saved, in her opinion, thousands, perhaps millions of children from devoting the same number of hours that it took them to devour such an imaginative story from what they might have normally spent watching television or playing video games. Elinor wanted to say, "I wonder what the Christian community has to say about you taking up the whole city block?" very politely of course, but instead she said, "Why doesn't the Christian community attack something really threatening like *Dexter's Laboratory* for example? Where are the outraged mothers banding together against the *Powerpuff Girls* or those fairies?"

"What's wrong with *Dexter* or the *Powerpuff Girls*?" Grace wanted to know.

"It's rubbish," she said.

"No it's not," Grace said, as if there was something wrong with her. "They're funny."

"No, they're not," Elinor insisted. "And they're not for kids. And in contrast to a wonderfully imaginative story like *Harry Potter*, they are loud, violent and obnoxious, and even a little creepy."

"Well, perhaps you're right. They do use a particular kind of irony that's often targeted at an adult audience, but I think they're hilarious."

Is that *irony* that they're using? Elinor wondered.

"Is the comedy intended for adults, then? Like Elmer in the paste-eating episode?" she asked.

The debate was beginning to heat up. And Stephanie was anxious to retreat, rather awestruck by the strange turn the conversation had taken from her mild cautioning to Elinor's wildly unwarranted attacks on *Dexter* and the *Powerpuff Girls*. You could see her frantically searching her own experience with *Dexter* and the *Powerpuff Girls* for what she might find so offensive in them. Perhaps Elinor was right, Stephanie was undoubtedly considering, that there possibly was something evil, satanic even, in that weird monkey Mojo Jojo. She had probably even sensed it herself but, as they all did, had given in to her children's demands to watch it.

"What's even worse is *SpongeBob SquarePants*," Deborah said.

"It's true," said Grace. After all she was the one among them most recently arrived from the States. "They're in the same category of a more stylized cartoon that's very popular now in some of these new kids cartoons," she informed, using the word "stylized" as if they had never heard of such a thing.

It was true. Elinor would have never even known about *Dexter* or the *Powerpuff Girls* if Alexi and Clara had not insisted on watching it every morning with her sister's kids while they were visiting over the holidays in the States. It was perhaps harmless enough, but she loved to bring it up as an example of a very bad influence.

"Well, it's the stupidest thing I've ever seen. My kids watched it all summer at home, and I couldn't stand it," Deborah said.

"Now, nothing's wrong with *SpongeBob SquarePants*," Grace corrected with authority. "It's very funny, although you're right, some of the humor is aimed at a more mature audience, but I see nothing wrong with that." She went on to say that SpongeBob was really a terrific character and possibly even role model as he teaches children that being a ninny can in fact triumph over bullies or the other snotty little cartoon characters that populated his ocean world. She began to tell of the scenario of one of the episodes.

"Now is this all happening under the sea?" Elinor asked. She was fascinated by her enthusiasm.

"Yes."

"And is SpongeBob a natural sponge or . . . ?"

"He's an industrialized sponge, synthetic and square, which of course emphasizes the irony of having him live in the ocean with a number of other ordinary sea creatures," she instructed as she continued to tell the story of how by being such a silly but friendly little sponge, SpongeBob had encouraged all the other sea creatures to welcome graciously rather than reject and make fun of all of the fat and obnoxious humans that populated their beaches.

"Well, I still don't get how being stupid and goofy ends up being a noble characteristic," Deborah said with a finality that must have offended Grace's proper opinion because she surprised the whole company by saying, "Maybe you don't like *SpongeBob SquarePants*, because you don't *get SpongeBob SquarePants*," which is really what she meant the whole time she had been defending the miserable little sponge anyway. Everyone was quiet.

The talk turned quickly to nostalgia for Sunday school, subdivisions, Chinese take-out and Katie Couric. Deborah wished for a drive through dry cleaner that would starch her husband's shirts as they certainly should be in his profession, and longed to be on the soccer field on Saturdays with all her other girlfriends at home and find a take-out café that knew how to make real *lattes*. Deborah had a great talent for hitting on the issues they faced and a way of filling up awkward silences with her practiced monologues.

"Molly begins to think that soccer is a *boy's* game," was her complaint that generally got the kind of horrified sympathy she was looking for. Elinor had heard her say it hundreds of times.

Grace commented on the color Deborah had chosen for her living room by saying, "Right before we moved, I'd just painted my dining room almost the exact same color. It was called butter cream. And you can imagine that was the perfect name to describe it, too, because it was so rich, I used to sit in there and just want to lick my walls."

Elinor stared at her in wonder.

Grace said that her bathroom wallpaper at home had an enormous red Georgia O'Keefe flower pattern on it.

"You know," she said, "it's like walking into a room filled with hundreds of vaginas."

Stephanie was horrified. Even Elinor was slightly uncomfortable.

"What do you mean?" Stephanie asked shocked. Vaginas and sex were topics better left unexplored—an unpleasant consequence to being a woman and the otherwise respectable state of marriage, and Stephanie was able to face them both only with resolve and determination. She avoided the issue as much as she could.

"You know, Georgia O'Keefe, the artist who paints the big flowers in precise detail." Stephanie still looked confused.

"Always big red flowers, real close up. Well, her paintings of flowers have always been interpreted as being very labial, like a vagina."

Stephanie was visibly horrified. Grace was choosing this topic expressly to horrify Stephanie and as a way of conveying her thorough and broad education.

"You know Stephanie, it's just one of those things. For some people it's just a big red flower. For others, it's a vagina. It's all in how you choose to view it," Deborah said.

"You have to wonder about people who understand this and yet insist upon decorating their house with it anyway," Deborah continued. "I guess in the end, it is all a matter of taste. Some people choose to decorate their house with religious icons, and some people choose to decorate their walls with flowers that look like vaginas. It's all a manner of personal expression."

"*You* haven't been to my house yet, Elinor?" Grace said, undaunted.

"No. No, I haven't," she said. On what occasion might she have been to her house? Grace hadn't been in France a month. "You're near Karen, I think?"

"Yes, if you go right up the street, past Karen's, further up the hill and off to the left, we're in the cul de sac at the very top."

"Well then, you have a very nice view," Elinor said.

"Oh, yes. It's wonderful! It's a marvelous view. It really is a remarkable view! We were very lucky." At this she paused, hoping not to appear immodest. "God has been good to us."

"Ah? Excellent."

"I wish I had chosen a view," Stephanie said wistfully, turning to gaze out the window of Deborah's living room.

"Yes, well, Elinor, you will need to come over, of course. In fact you *have* to come over. I need your advice on something. I'm thinking of putting drapes in the *salle de séjour*. You see I have two sets of sliding glass doors, side by side, that look out over the *cathédrale*, and I think I may have found the perfect thing. Bill says we should do something sheer, so that you can still enjoy the view through the curtains."

"Certainly," she said. Elinor couldn't think why Grace should need her opinion on something that sounded so perfect.

"And what does your husband do?" Stephanie asked. It was always important for Stephanie to know what everyone's husband did, as *she* had nothing to recommend herself other than her own husband's job.

"He's in marketing," who, she went on to say, was responsible for developing and implementing a customer loyalty program at Durtol. A concept virtually unknown to the French.

"He started out in advertising. He wrote jingles for TV commercials," she laughed. "He majored in music theory. He comes from a very musical family. Now I don't know how familiar you are with advertising or how commercials are made," she continued, "but, it's very much like making a movie—with writers, composers, producers and directors."

"So your husband's a composer?" Elinor asked.

"Well, yes," she said as if pleased with the idea of it herself.

"A composer of jingles?"

"He comes from a *very* musical family."

"I see."

Stephanie said, "Well, you certainly know a great deal about what your husband does. I never know exactly what it is my husband does."

"Oh?" Grace said. "I think I have a very good idea of what your husband does."

Grace was eager to conspire with Stephanie in their similarly low expectations of what life could offer them in France, although they were both eager to be viewed as so open and accepting of the diversity of the world only with the confirmed satisfaction in their own superiority.

Elinor was startled at her assumptions, the general assuming nature of *all* the American women she stood among, gathered around Deborah's dining room table full of pastry baked from Bisquick, talking of the near absence of drive through service, take-out coffee, and Corian countertops, and the persistently assumed superiority and fast efficiency of the States. They refused to pay any attention at all to France, to even watch French television or to get it on their elaborate satellite entertainment systems. Or, worse, Grace who had not been here a month, yet was an immediate expert on France and the French. It was impossible to claim an understanding of something so beautiful, mysterious and allusive, even after nearly three years of living among these people, Elinor never seemed to get to know them or understand all their contradictions. She finished the chocolate chip coffee cake that everyone had been raving about, slung down the last of Deborah's bland coffee and escaped.

10

Elinor began to feel foreign among the members of her own culture and inaccessible to the French who were naturally suspicious of her lively American-ness which is always threatening to the French who refuse to admire it or enthusiastically import it as other cultures do. But that was indeed the allure of the French—their indifference or refusal to be particularly agreeable. She began to understand that they prefer no one's company so much as their own, living so much more within themselves, knowing better how to please themselves, practicing a particular social behavior when necessary but never feeling fully comfortable in the company of others—an attitude that comes across as being arrogant or selfish but indeed is truly rather self-conscious around anyone unknown to them. They also tend to smoke incessantly, blowing a hazy cloud of smoke between each other as extra protection. It also casts a soft-focus around themselves which serves to screen out any other of their imperfections. The women—*that woman*, particularly—seemed to be as determined to hate Elinor as she was curious about her, for Elinor began to know of a mutual fascination between them.

There seemed to be such an effort made by the other French women at the school to ignore the expatriates, afraid they might not speak French, afraid of their spontaneity and enthusiasm and always envious of their white teeth. French women have never been allowed to develop much of a sense of humor or to take themselves very lightly at all. Many of their attempts at humor are at the expense of others, for they find it very difficult to be honest enough about being themselves ridiculous, which is essential for being funny. Self-deprecation is unheard of and impossible to carry off in a culture so concerned with elegance and savoir faire. That is why when the truth about themselves is revealed or shared, it takes on a precious sincerity that is lacking in the steady stream of wise-cracks for example that Deborah was so skilled at.

Pierre Durtol, a little boy in Clara's class and likely heir to the Durtol empire, invited Clara to his birthday party. The formal invitation came home in her *cartable*. It looked like a wedding announcement, with the date, time, address and a number to call to RSVP. Elinor was very sur-prised. It seemed to be a great accomplishment, a compliment or reflec-tion of the progress they had made to speak French or be recognized as making that effort anyway. She accepted straight away and enjoyed a great deal searching for the apartment through the twisting allies of the city *centre*. Clara, too, seemed to enjoy the adventure. Cherbourg was filled with dark and narrow alleys with ancient wooden doorways that led up to pleasant enough apartments above the street. As they turned onto the narrow street that was marked on the invitation, Elinor ran nearly face first into the breasts of an enormous prostitute, although it was only three o'clock in the afternoon. The woman looked like a truck driver in a black bustier, tight miniskirt and thigh boots. Elinor knew she was a woman somehow, even though for a French woman she was enormous.

"Voulez-vous venir chez moi?" the woman asked. Elinor gasped, although Clara didn't bat an eye.

They found the heavy gate with one large red balloon tied to the great iron pull swaying on its tether to and fro as if beckoning to them. Elinor was thrilled with the quest of walking up the stone stairs worn shiny and hewn with use to Madame Durtol's apartment as discreet and private as she was herself, nothing like the Manhattan apartments the wealthy American industrialists might have. Because who knew that people, the Durtols, dwelt here behind the black stone of the facades of these buildings that only seemed to wall in the many passageways that snaked through the city in a kind of labyrinth that inevitably ended up at the great black cathedral. Everyone lived above stairs it seemed.

When Elinor walked into the elegant apartment filled with little children and their mommies stylishly dressed and vaguely familiar to her from the school, she couldn't help being satisfied in the idea that they were not so much unlike her as to get together in their own leisurely lives for coffee and chat, watching their children play, helping with birthday parties. These women, whose children attended private Catholic school, rarely worked. Elinor saw Elisabeth and Antoine among the children, and she looked up around the room for their mommy.

There *she* sat in the gloom of the rainy day, smoking elegantly. The beautiful Frenchwoman had taken off her coat, but she was still wearing her scarf as if poised for flight, like some beautiful deer. They acknowledged each other immediately, although made no move to greet one another. Elinor immediately recognized she was the only American there and thus a point of interest and curiosity. Madame Durtol moved about pouring her out a dainty cup of black coffee and offering her cream and sugar.

American girls are not so graceful and elegant as French women are, but they *are* healthy, handsome, and athletic, which is enough to make French women very ill at ease, cautious, and curious at the same time. There was an awkward hesitation but a marked interest in making conversation, and they asked Elinor the usual questions about her living in France. For when you say that you are American, the words curl up under their nose like a tantalizing bouquet of a tempting dish. *"Ah,"* they say, America, the land of dreams, where *tout est possible*—the New World, where Elvis is from and everyone drinks Coca Cola.

They tried to carry on amongst each other in the natural way that they might, making reference to the obvious differences in how she might view whatever was being said. They seemed always to be self-conscious—an affected behavior that never lets down its guard. Elinor could feel the Frenchwoman's interest in her as she moved to join the conversation. There was already such a feeling of knowing each other that it did not seem at all out of the ordinary for the woman to approach and remark directly in French on how she liked the coffee.

"*Les Americains*, they drink it like water in such enormous cups." The comment was designed to demonstrate their lack of taste. And Elinor could only agree reluctantly that it was true. The woman began to tell of how she and her husband had visited the States one summer and traveled from New York to Chicago in an old Chevy. "Everyone else had air conditioning and a fancy car, so enormous and inefficient."

"Ah bon?" was Elinor's bemused reply. Nothing could be so gauche as to drive a fancy car.

She asked directly where Elinor lived, and when she said in Cezallier, the woman recounted how just after she had moved to Cherbourg, she had gotten lost "out there"—implying the provinces.

"I was trying to go out there to the supermarket and went round about the *rond-point* and got off in Cezallier. It seems very nice, very like a suburban neighborhood," she said trying to sound polite, but there was a mild sting to her tone, in her attitude.

"It is right by the Centre Commercial," she informed the other ladies, "very convenient. Americans love convenience and size. I suppose you could never be convinced to live in an apartment in town?"

"Not with four children," Elinor returned with a sincere smile, "I was clever enough to have only two."

The woman laughed at herself, it seemed, for her own aggressiveness.

"And your husband? He works for Durtol? Why does he never bring the children in to school?" she asked, displaying openly her curiosity. It seemed she might have known a great deal more about Elinor than was natural.

"He does. Have you never seen him?"

"Peut être," she said interested. "What does he look like?"

"Beau, intelligent et il est à moi," Elinor said with bravado. One can imagine how difficult it was for her to keep up with the conversation,

defend herself as she felt she must certainly do, and appear at ease in a foreign language among people who puzzled and fascinated her at the same time. And you needed a great deal of spit to wet your lips enough to carry on a conversation in French for any length of time. But Elinor wanted to talk to her. More than anything, she wanted to listen to her voice, hear what she said. She was terribly interested.

Madame Durtol came into the salon with a lump of *fromage fermier* she was raving about and insisted they all taste. She said she had bought it at the market and began a long description of the qualities that made it such a superior cheese—how long it had been aged, the particular culture, salt, etc. In France, even salt comes in numerous varieties. Elinor was always amazed by the meticulous appreciation the French had and how they could go on about the varieties and quality of something as straightforward as cheese, which in the States usually came down to white or yellow. It made her think of the plastic food that came with Clara's toy kitchen she had gotten for Christmas. There was a little lump of white plastic that was supposed to be *gaperon* cheese. Elinor had looked at it and wondered if it might be mistaken for something else by Americans, for instance, who would be unfamiliar with it. Was it supposed to be a sponge, ice cream, pale scrambled eggs or tofu?

The plastic food included other gourmet items, like, garlic and eschalot, leeks, marinated fish and olives. The little children could concoct these ingredients in a stylish miniature stainless steel soup pot on the commercial-style stove and stir it up with a variety of exotic whisks and wooden spatulas.

Madame Durtol went on to say how the cheese should be sampled on plain white water crackers or sliced baguette, not to interfere too much with the enjoyment of the cheese itself and at what temperature it should be stored.

"But Madame, you haven't told us who was the cow that produced such a marvelous cheese?" the beautiful Frenchwoman said, with a faint smile on her lips, poking a bit of fun at the elaborate explanation. There was a collective tittering of laughter as the other women appreciated the joke. Elinor did, too, and was astonished that the woman could be funny.

It was almost as if she understood that Elinor might think the explanation excessive, and the French never like to be thought frivolous.

"How old is your other daughter?" the woman asked.

"Alexi a cinquante." Elinor said that Alexi was *fifty* years old, erring in her uneasiness, ending the word with a consonant sound as speakers of English are inclined to do instead of *cinq ans*—five, the end sound left open but with a nasal finish to it. She recovered, correcting herself. They tolerated it well enough.

"And she just learned to drive—*je veux dire*—ride her bike over the weekend," she added, just to demonstrate her alacrity.

What was it like to live in France, the woman asked for the benefit of the other women, who were curious as well. Elinor told the truth. That it was lovely, although her life was perhaps a little superficial. She would naturally have to work if she were back in the States, she assured them. Her life of luxury and her ability to enjoy France and her children was based on the advantages of being an expatriate.

"And what is your work?" the woman asked with interest. These were all topics and avenues they could take to have a conversation.

Elinor said that she was an English teacher. The woman mentioned how she loved Steinbeck and Henry James—*Le Tourne d'Ecrou*, she said, and then complimented her on her French, although was ready to correct her, and asked how the children were getting along in French.

"Elles comprennent bien. Presque tout. They understand a great deal, most in fact, and they begin to speak at home to each other in French," was her reply.

"Don't you speak to them at home in French?" the woman asked innocently. Elinor was surprised by the question. What seemed so natural to her was in fact enormously complex and difficult for Elinor. She and Victor rarely spoke French at home and only for the benefit of the children. It would make things far too complicated and artificial, when their relationship had never started or developed in French. Not to mention that French seemed to lack the playful teasing always present in what they said in English. It seemed so formal, precise and articulate. It was never funny or after a laugh.

She did sometimes, Elinor said, in the supermarket or when they were in the company of other French friends. But French, the language, seemed never very natural or suited to the relationship she had with her children, she explained. When she thought of it, Elinor realized that she usually used it to scold them lightly, or remind them of their manners, *"qu'est-ce que tu dis?"* To remind them to greet their friends, their teacher, to say please, thank you or good-bye, or to explain what something was that they only knew in French. It was quite difficult to know what it was they had done at school unless they spoke a bit in French—their entire school day was happening in French, and they had not the vocabulary to tell her of it in English.

Madame Durtol, who had lived for some time with her husband in the States, apologized in French for her dreadful English.

"Vous devez m'excuser. Even though I lived in the States years ago, I could only just get by."

A discussion began on how inadequate was everyone's English. And how they had all hated their English teachers in school. If there is anyone made more relentless fun of on French television, it is the stereotypical French English professor who insists on speaking to her students entirely in English while the French high school students roll their eyes and disregard anything she says as if she is a babbling lunatic.

The beautiful Frenchwoman said that her father was an archaeologist and that she had traveled all over the world from Egypt to Guatemala. Her husband was a professor at the university and they had lived abroad for several years in Algeria and in Egypt where she said she spoke English, although she made no attempt to do so now.

"We lived very simply, but with four children in school, he decided to come back to France."

"My English is dreadful too," Elinor said, *"mais, j'ai pas d'accent."* The women all stared at her, afraid to suspect she might be joking.

"And your husband is Romanian?"

"Ben oui," she answered quickly, feeling momentarily defensive. Although Victor was indeed American now, his barbaric ancestry would certainly place him in a culturally inferior category. And Elinor began to suspect the woman's questions tended to serve some curiosity if she might

be her equal in terms of status and education, thus allowing them the opportunity to even begin to be friends. The woman drew closer to her and said, *"Ca te rend interessante.* That makes you very interesting."

Elinor studied her curiously. She noticed the woman had *tutoyered* her very naturally as if they had known each other for ages, or at least for the half an hour she had been at the party anyway. "You don't seem like you wish to stay among the other Americans—that you married a Romanian and that you're interested in . . ." here she stopped herself, but Elinor could almost finish her sentence by what was implied in her look—"that you would be interested in a French girl like me." But instead the woman had some change of feeling and said, "that you make such an effort to speak French. The other Americans don't seem to make the slightest effort. Except of course Catherine Mort de Froy," she said raising an eyebrow. *"Son Francais est excellent.* She speaks perfectly, without an accent."

"Oui, tout a fait," Elinor acknowledged reluctantly.

"She doesn't like me at all," the woman said abruptly as if she wanted to hurry and defend herself from any gossip or slander that might damage or influence Elinor's opinion of her. "We used to get along very well. I talked to her often, in fact. She even invited me to her home for dinner, which was nice. Her husband is French, you know. My husband and I went, but after that, for no apparent reason at all, she stopped talking to me. She doesn't acknowledge me at all. Walks by as if she's never seen me in her life," she laughed awkwardly.

Elinor flushed, as if the woman were referring to how she had refused to acknowledge her just after they met. It struck her as interesting that the woman should be bothered by this. The aloofness she exuded gave her immunity to being snubbed and made her seem indifferent to belonging or having any women friends at all. The idea that this woman might feel the pain of not being noticed, included or invited was unfathomable. But the reason for Catherine's contempt was obvious. It was the woman's beauty that infuriated her, made her jealous perhaps at dinner, possessive of her husband. Elinor was well acquainted with the female inclination to hate other women for being beautiful.

"You are a beautiful woman and naturally she hates you for that," Elinor said directly. The woman stared at her. It was not as if she were surprised, or didn't know this to be true herself. It was that she never expected to be told it so matter-of-factly and by a woman.

Clara came running up and grabbed Elinor around the leg.

"What're you up to, puppy?" she asked in English which seemed an awkward reminder of their differences. The woman smiled as one does when children are present and crouched down to look at Clara.

"Clara is very charming. *J'adore tes yeux,*" she said, "Are they green, or blue, like your mother's?" She flashed a grin up at Elinor. The attention seemed an opportunity to pay her a compliment as Elinor had done, but the strange familiarity was unmistakable, fascinatingly inappropriate, speaking of Clara's eyes as if she had studied her child with the same intense curiosity Elinor had studied the woman's children's faces to discover something of her. What a strange thing to understand and take such pains to deny, as they both had done so carefully, revealing nothing of this secret to anyone, least of all their husbands, who would think them ridiculously childish for entertaining such a crush.

Elinor let Clara go, and they joined the rest of the group. The talk had turned to how white Americans' teeth are and did they use some kind of cosmetic.

The Frenchwoman assured the others that this was no great accomplishment, and that even the more savage cultures, such as Nigerians, had wonderfully white teeth, naturally and without the aid of a cosmetic. She had lived in Nigeria.

"It's the fluoride. They put fluoride in the water in the States," one of the women said. "They fluoridate the water in America. I read about it in a magazine."

"That's why Americans are so easygoing," someone else agreed. She went on to say that fluoride had a sedating effect and that it killed brain cells. Naturally, it was the reason why Americans were not as clever or intellectual as the French and why they spoke an inferior language, bereft of the kind of richness of subtly and expression of French, *La Belle Langue*. Fluoride was a plot by the government to sedate the population and keep them stupid. But Americans did have beautiful teeth, but that didn't matter because they all had plastic surgery and liposuction anyway, and how was Elinor so *très sportive* and fit? They were also all convinced that cellulite could be removed with magical creams and potions found at the pharmacy.

Before the party ended, Elinor asked the Frenchwoman, "I'm sorry but, I don't know your name?" It seemed very strange that they should continue in this way without ever knowing each other's names. It is after all, something Americans generally exchange right away.

"Béatrice," the woman said.

"Je suis Elinor," she said.

"Je sais," the woman said, regarding her intently.

11

The woman's name was Béatrice Deveux and together they left the apartment with their children, standing for a moment on the street below.

"Pourquoi tu ne viens pas prendre un café chez moi? Why don't you come to my apartment for a coffee?" the woman asked. "I just live a few blocks from here. My husband has taken the girls to their lessons in town and is out for the rest of the afternoon."

"Why, yes. Thank you very much," Elinor said with sudden excitement, and she took Clara by the hand and followed the woman and the twins through the narrow street. They said practically nothing to each other. Elinor began to think and anticipate something in the invitation and suddenly wished to flee—the apartment couldn't possibly be just a few blocks away. She had to adjust her walk, which was normally rather quick, to the slow gait of the French woman.

As they turned onto Rue de la Boucherie, they stopped in front of a Parisian-looking apartment building from the turn of the century.

"Come on up, it's the third floor," which in France always seemed like the fourth floor because no one ever lives on the first floor. It's for bicycles, motor scooters, *poussettes* or the concierge. Elinor followed her and the children up the winding staircase, and they stood at the door, waiting for Béatrice to unlock the door. There was an awkward pause and then she stepped aside to let Elinor in, and they stood together in the entrée. Elinor released Clara to follow the twins back through the apartment to play. So close, Béatrice appeared a little frightening to her, with her hair pulled back into a knot at the back. Larger than life and so beautiful, she was hard to look at. They avoided it. It seemed difficult to look directly at one another.

The day was rather cool, but it was hot and stuffy in the apartment. Béatrice apologized, "It smells of mold," she said. "It's in the carpets, I can't seem to get rid of it," she apologized, leading Elinor into the salon. She opened the French doors onto the terrace, to let in some air and show her the bleak view into an airshaft. She seemed ashamed and eager to prove the disadvantages of the apartment. She lit a cigarette.

The apartment was exactly as Elinor might have imagined it would be with Persian rugs everywhere. If they were not on the floor, they decorated the walls. Other bits of Persian embroidered tapestries hung about the high baroque ceilings which gave the impression of being in a tent in the desert. It was a narrow space divided into four bedrooms, a kitchen, bath, and a *salle de sejour* she had furnished with enormous family pieces she had inherited, she said, leaning up against the walls as if waiting for a table in a crowded restaurant.

The apartment had two bay windows on the east side and in one sat a birdcage with two *perroquets,* Romeo and Juliette, she said, and in the other, a little female tortoise, named Coquette. Romeo and Juliette had a baby, Béatrice told her, that died a few days ago, and there was another egg in the nest. But Juliette preferred to sit on the swing with her mate and didn't seem very interested in the egg, so she didn't have much hope.

"It was a big baby," she said, "almost as big as Romeo. But, I suppose it died from being in the sun. I guess I wasn't careful enough. I didn't always cover the cage. They can die of things like that, you know—*un courant d'air, ou le soleil.* Although we've had them for three years, at the beginning you have to be very careful, keep the cage covered, and I never let the children go very near the cage." Elinor didn't know how that was possible with four children in such a small space. "They can die of fright, you know, just like that. We've lost about three others before who only lived a few weeks or a month or two."

"But they must be rather happy then, to make a baby," Elinor said awkwardly.

"Oh, yes," she said, "they live much longer with a companion. They can die of loneliness too, I suppose," she said and then smiled a melancholic smile.

She stood smoking, and Elinor took off her jacket, commenting on the carpets and embroideries that decorated the apartment.

"They had wonderful bazaars in Algiers, selling silver jewelry, lapis lazuli, Middle Eastern broderis, amber, and superb tapestries and carpets. *C'était les milles et une nuit* and perhaps I enjoyed it too much. Am I talking too fast?" she interrupted herself, and Elinor said no. In the living room, she had a funky *canapé* covered with pillows near a low table and she pulled out some absurd, certainly Middle Eastern chair and offered it to her, apologizing that she didn't have much furniture. Elinor sat down into it, nearly knocking herself in the chin with her knees, and Béatrice went to make the coffee. Elinor could hardly get over the implausibility of her situation. She was in this woman's untidy apartment with nutty Persian carpets on the floor and hairbrushes tangled with her daughters' hair on the living room table.

When Béatrice returned, Elinor said, "Tell me about Algiers."

"Ah," she said, regarding her suspiciously, questioning her true interest in the subject. "That's an experience that's left a profound impression that stays with me, and I cannot forget." Again she eyed Elinor with the curious look to see if she would still be interested. Elinor stared back, waiting.

"It's a place so completely strange and foreign, incomparable with Europe or even with other countries of the world." She had already told Elinor that her father was an archaeologist, and she had lived in Guatemala, India and Egypt.

"It was very difficult to live in a place without any of our natural points of reference, to endure the condition of women, the prevailing misery and deprivation. It's like a place untouched by modern civilization." She told her that her husband taught Agricultural Science at the university in 1990.

"It was a dangerous voyage, where we often had to conceal our identity. This was at a time when foreigners, most particularly the French, were at risk. Our occupation of their country had created enormous hostility toward the French, although they're thoroughly influenced by French culture. My husband accepted to teach there to help them, but it's true, after Naomi, came along, I found it very hard to bear, to suffer being a women there, where one must be hidden all the time, cannot look directly in a man's eyes, and must be careful of every movement or gesture. It was insupportable. But it's an experience that I recall nearly every day."

She talked of how hard it was for her children at school and some of the hostility they encountered on the playground and the difficulty of day-to-day life, conditions that in Elinor's privileged life she couldn't begin to relate to, which made her contemplate their differences. Elinor was inclined to be bored with women who suffered, or were excessively compassionate, or dramatic. In the eighties she had never much liked to date the young men who camped out on the quad in protest of Apartheid or some other injustice. In the city, she had dated some such tortured artist for several weeks in which he dragged her relentlessly around to art openings and exhibits that she was more or less repulsed by, determined to discover something in him that would match his good looks, but at last, she could not manage to be interested in the music he listened to, the clubs he took her to, or in any of his opinions, which were always vastly general and compromising. In short, she had always been suspicious of earnestness. Now she listened intently, marveling at Béatrice's experience, although dramatic, it did seem real and she felt suddenly silly in her own bourgeois life.

Béatrice got up and went into the hall, and then came back with a dark blue bundle. Smiling shyly, she unfolded it and said, "This is it. This is the burqa I wore." And she threw it over herself and stood looking at Elinor from behind the handwoven netting that covered her face. Elinor was startled and stared at her as if she might have just taken a razor to her head and shaved off her hair in a rebellious passion to destroy her beauty. There she stood, nothing but a black ghost. She could have been a piece of furniture, covered to be put in the attic, or an overcoat hanging on a rack in the corner. Béatrice moved toward her like a phantom, and Elinor instinctively drew back, speechless. Elinor imagined she would have to pick up a phone like a prisoner to talk to her from behind the thing. Béatrice took it off as quickly as she had put it on and held it limp in her hand.

"It was exhausting, you see. I preferred to hide behind this than to be always watched or cheated in the marketplace."

Elinor looked at it fixedly. Béatrice had certainly demonstrated the effectiveness of its design. It had made her disappear, like a satin hand-kerchief in a sleight of hand—all her beauty, grace and spirit were silenced behind a curtain of death. Elinor believed she had never known the privilege of freedom until Béatrice showed her slavery and invisibility so quietly.

The way in which Béatrice discussed her past was open and honest, yet cautious and suspicious as if there was something she would not hazard. "It's possible that we may leave again. My husband despises routine and loves adventure. He's always accepting to do research or student development projects abroad. The university encourages professors to teach abroad. It enlarges their goals and spreads the French way, which is always very rational and *raisonable*," she said, smiling. "My husband enjoys being influential and working with young people. I also think he just likes the challenge and novelty of adapting to different cultures." Elinor said nothing and followed her into the kitchen with the coffee cups.

"Is your husband like that? I mean, does he like his work?" Béatrice asked.

"Yes, I suppose he does," Elinor said. It was true or at least he never complained, anyway.

"What about you?" Elinor asked. "Do you like moving around, living abroad?"

"It's interesting of course, but it's not so easy with the children. I suppose I always wanted to travel and see the world. Luc was so ambitious and exciting. He wanted to take me with him, show me all these places, but with the children it's never easy to adjust to a different life all the time. Sometimes I just wish we could be like everyone else, content to stay at home, except to visit the grandparents, you know, like everyone else." She smiled. "Sometimes, I suppose I feel like my children don't know where they belong, certainly not in France."

Elinor raised her eyebrows, "Yes, I know what you mean."

"It's impossible that they should feel French, we've spent such little time here. Luc is not interested in staying. He already knows France, he's married to a French woman, nothing could be more ordinary," she said laughing.

Elinor nodded, not knowing what to say. Absently she admired a photograph on the refrigerator of Béatrice on a hillside. She was standing astride a bicycle with little Elisabeth on the child seat in back.

"Where's this?" she asked.

"That's actually in France. *C'est rigolo*," Béatrice said, explaining that she and Luc were always searching out interesting things to do with the kids in the region. *"C'est vers les Alps*. It's a national park you can rent bicycles and ride them on the trails near the lake. Some people take it very seriously, and you can even camp along the way."

Béatrice looked so strong and beautiful in the picture. Elinor suddenly asked her if she could have it.

"Yes, if you like," she said, removing it and giving it to her. Elinor suddenly felt an impropriety in their abrupt intimacy. After all they didn't know each other so well. This sudden awareness made Elinor feel awkward and alert, as if she must be very careful with it and behave herself. Béatrice went to search for the brochure of the place, saying Elinor ought to try it herself. Elinor followed her back into the living room.

Béatrice found what she was looking for right away in a file box at the bottom of one of the bookcases.

"I can't believe I was able to find it in all this mess," she said gesturing to the books in stacks on the floor about the room. She handed it to Elinor and then bent to sit on the piano bench near the bookshelf. Elinor watched her run her hands over her hips to her knees, bending to sit, arching her back slightly to stare up at her. Elinor thrilled at the grace of the gesture. Here was another woman whose charms did not inspire envy or contempt. The lovely curve of her hips seemed so sweet that Elinor could not suppress a strange rush of desire. Suddenly, Béatrice reached out and ran her two fingers down the paint stain Elinor had on the hip of her jeans and rested them there for a moment. Elinor was startled and embarrassed by her touch.

"It's paint," she said awkwardly.

Slowly, Béatrice let her hand fall away, looking up at Elinor with her sad smile. What did she want her to do? Elinor was so confused. But why shouldn't she want to reach out and touch her, express in the best way she knew how the intention of her notice? Béatrice, who was so used to being beautiful and seductive, understood her power and wanted it to work on Elinor, perhaps so she could escape some loneliness she felt. They both were fascinated by their sudden intimacy when they really knew nothing at all of each other.

"Tu trembles," Béatrice said, half with a smile and stood as if disappointed or rejected. It was true, Elinor realized, feeling suddenly prudish and chaste. They stood facing each other with very little space between them. Elinor stood rooted with fear. She could not think what would happen next. Virtually alone in the apartment, except for the presence of the children, in a normal domestic setting without even a language in common but perhaps with everything else in common, Elinor wanted to ask her what was happening, what the secret was that they shared. But she was too afraid to learn the truth of this longing or that it was nothing, except two women having coffee while their children played in the apartment.

"Well, I'd better be going," Elinor said awkwardly. "Victor will wonder where I've gotten to." Béatrice stood and pressed her lips together in a smile. Elinor went silently to get Clara to go, and Béatrice walked them to the door.

"Thank you," Elinor said, feeling somehow disappointed. *"C'etait gentil.* It was very kind of you to invite us."

"Yes, thank you for coming," Béatrice said, and then leaned in very close and kissed her gently on the cheek. Elinor was stunned and slowly turned her head to offer her other cheek in the customary *bisou* exchanged between friends. But the normally benign kiss that she was accustomed to exchange between her other acquaintances was unexpected, and Elinor was so startled that she nearly forgot to offer her other cheek which would have been a disaster. She turned with Clara down the stairs frightened and delighted with the kiss.

On Thursday afternoon when they arrived at the school to pick up the kids, Béatrice approached Elinor as enthusiastically as a child and kissed her in greeting on each cheek and handed her a bag of apricots and another bag of about four of Elisabeth's little dresses and *pantalons* for Clara. Americans generally suspect the French of being more sophisticated, clever and aloof than they are. After all, they all speak French—sophisticated and urbane in itself. But sometimes they reveal themselves to be very open, easy and sincere, with a wonderful childlike delight in the simplest things.

"Thank you for coming to my house the other day," she said, and Elinor peered into the little sack with the dresses in it. "I've been going through all the girls' things, and Elisabeth has already outgrown these, but I think they might still fit Clara." Elinor felt a tender heaving of her heart, looking at the sweet little dresses and the apricots. She said thank you and acted as if it had not moved her any more than usual. They walked to the gate in pleasant chat about the weekend, and Elinor felt a childish rush of feeling in loving her new friend.

The sun had taken on a new slant, and the weather warmed. Concealed in the gloom of March, spring crept stealthily over the countryside, bringing it to life with color and dotting it with bright red poppies, as if touched by an artist's brush or a fairy's wand—brilliant and already in bloom by April. In the early evenings you could hear the earth awakening with life—the insects humming, the crickets singing, the very ground pulsating, throbbing like the beating of a heart. Elinor had been practicing slowing down. She tried to do things with the extra attention she admired so much in the French, Béatrice particularly. She began to cook more deliberately, enjoying everything she did—going to the market to pick out her ingredients, washing and chopping the vegetables, presenting it nicely, making her own dressings and sauces instead of dashing together something that would go with a *poulet roti* she had picked up at the Rotisserie. They started eating a family lunch—*dejeuner*—on the weekends outside in the sun, taking their time, she and Victor drinking wine with the meal and talking.

She took more pleasure in doing things like bathing the children, brushing their hair, and dressing their little bodies. She kissed them on the lips, knowing that she was being indulgent, but she didn't care. It was better to kiss something so young and alive than not. She even tried to adopt Béatrice's luxurious walk toward the gate with her children. It was strange and foreign to Elinor not to fling the children out of the car and scramble to the gate, strapping the girls into their *cartables* and then hurrying them with encouragement. "Go on Alexi, run on ahead," she would say while she dragged Clara by the hand. There wasn't room enough on the narrow sidewalk for all three of them. It all took an actual effort because this kind of deliberate pleasure in routine did not come naturally. She had to consciously tell herself to slow down and try to stroll toward the gate as if she might be taking the air with them rather than hauling the kids to school.

She had to wake up earlier to enjoy a light breakfast and coffee with her girls at the table now, and then they could leave in enough time so that they didn't have to rush to get to school.

Béatrice began coming to school in sneakers and sweat pants a couple days a week, which struck Elinor as a startling contrast to her usual French elegance and nicotine habit. The French feel no need to exert themselves in anyway, however, Béatrice told her she might have "to miss the gym today" as they stood in the corridor before dropping their little ones with their teacher, because little Antoine was fussing and complaining of a stomachache. Béatrice, she noticed, had her lovely brunette hair highlighted in auburn, which disappointed her.

12

In the afternoon when Elinor parked her car to pick up Alexi, she saw Béatrice waiting in her van. Elinor might have stopped and chatted if Béatrice were one of her American girlfriends but instead she pretended she didn't see her and continued with little Clara in tow toward the gate. She waited in the light sprinkle in the doorway, and when she saw Deborah and Grace approaching, she knew it was unavoidable that she must talk to them. She suddenly regretted not having the courage to stand at Béatrice's van and talk to her instead. Elinor even sensed Béatrice would have wanted her to. It was so silly really, this childish game they were playing. Elinor put it from her mind.

Deborah and Grace were wearing sneakers and sweat pants.

"We just finished this great step class!" Deborah announced enthusiastically. "The instructor is great. He really makes you work. My butt's killing me."

"Elinor, have you ever done step?" Grace interrupted. "Do you know what *step* is?" Before any of the discussion could continue, this point had to be established, because don't imagine step is anything so foolish as a bunch of mommies sweating to disco music. It is a far more specific and precise form of exercise than aerobics, its silly predecessor. And surely during Elinor's absence from the States, step had gained its popularity, and she was sure to be as unfamiliar with it as she was with *SpongeBob SquarePants*.

"No, Grace, I don't think I do," she said, momentarily interested in her explanation.

"Step is—" Grace began, but Elinor didn't stay to listen. She turned away from her in mid-sentence when she saw Béatrice approach with her slow gait, her beautiful head wrapped in a pale green scarf against the drizzle.

Elinor just left Deborah and Grace standing there, watching her turn away and walk up to the mysterious French woman as if compelled to do so.

"Béatrice," Elinor spoke her name, and Béatrice greeted her with warmth and a kind of relief that she would not be ignored.

"Ou sont les jumeaux?" She asked where the twins were, standing with Clara now in her arms for her protection against the rain. Béatrice had left them in the apartment with the *femme de ménage*. "It's much easier. You know I live just up the street," she said. It allowed her some relief, she said, to get out for a moment, smoke a cigarette and enjoy the walk back home with her older girls.

"Will you come up again for coffee?" Béatrice asked.

"Ben oui, bien sur."

It was unheard of, strange, and unprecedented that Elinor should want to talk to one of the Frenchwomen, especially one who had not returned from the States recently or spoke perfect English and attended all of their PTA meetings was all Elinor was sure Grace and Deborah could think as she felt their notice bearing down on her. Their surprise and indignation that she would simply step down from the curb and choose that Frenchwoman, looking so romantic with her head wrapped in the scarf like that, seemed apparent. Elinor became rather conscious of what kind of impression her behavior had made—on Deborah, who she knew was awed by such an affront. Elinor was surprised herself by her own behavior. Béatrice and she were not exactly friends and to be friends seemed so difficult given their circumstances. Elinor could compare this only to some retreat back to childhood, this desire, like schoolgirls saving each other a seat as a sign of their devotion. Elinor could hear Deborah telling Phil, her husband, "Elinor just ditched us and went up to talk to that beautiful Frenchwoman." She would despise her for it, think Elinor was trying to show off her proficiency in French to *her*. What else could possibly motivate Elinor to behave in such a way other than to display French friends as Deborah did her charming children? Unless suddenly it might occur to her. Elinor was sure her behavior and efforts to talk to Béatrice in the corridor before school had not gone unnoticed. No one spoke of it, but perhaps everyone had noticed it. The fact was that none of them mixed much with the Frenchwomen except for various particular reasons such as school activities or birthday parties for their children. None of the Frenchwomen, even the ones who spoke perfect English, ever came up to the café for a coffee after dropping off their children. Surely a question had been raised in Deborah's mind, in the minds of some of the other women, too. Maybe everyone knew and was laughing at her. It was perhaps obscene!

Suddenly she saw the realization, the flash of enlightenment, appear in Deborah's clever brain, "Elinor's in love with that woman."

She could hear her eventually posing the question to her with her *vache* unreserve, "I think you're in love with her, *Elinor*." To which she thought she must reply, "Yes, I think I am."

This fascination had carried on so long, started out so gradually, noticing each other, Elinor had gotten used to it. It could hardly be any different for Béatrice. Pretending not to notice each other but waiting in the corridor every morning with their children to exchange some sort of conversation, say anything, or notice each other's children at least.

In the afternoons while they waited for their older children to appear in the courtyard, although they said nothing, Béatrice would send Elisabeth and Antoine to play with Clara. They both used all their skills and charms to get the other's notice. Elinor knew even when they did become friends, they would never speak of it, confide in their intense desire to know each other that seemed so inevitable that when it happened there was some immediate intimacy.

Their attraction to one another had never been repulsive or disgusting In fact the very nature of its absurdity was thrilling, strange and mysterious. Elinor could not decide whether to be ashamed of her feelings or to embrace them as natural and just.

The idea that she could feel such passion for someone again in her life, be infatuated with the same intensity that one only experiences as a child or adolescent seemed wonderfully foolish, reckless and naive.

Elinor loved Victor, perhaps more than ever. They had such a comfortable joy in each other. He was truly her best friend and her lover, too. She remembered feeling the same sort of giddiness around him. Béatrice had the same gypsy beauty she had married Victor for, and she had been afraid of him, too. Now, Elinor's desire for him seemed so simple and easy, so natural and easy to comprehend. Elinor's desire for Béatrice, however was so unnatural and complex, it terrified her—made her almost panic.

Béatrice took out a pack of cigarettes from her purse, some cool ethnic woven thing, and offered her one. Elinor said no thank you. She could just imagine what kind of an impression that might make on the American ladies, watching her share a cigarette with Béatrice, like two rebellious teenagers hanging out in front of the school gate. Béatrice seemed surprised.

"Tu fume pas? You don't smoke?" she asked. All French women were at least closet smokers, even if they weren't out in the way Béatrice was.

"De temps en temps? Not ever?" she asked with disbelief.

"Well, I did sometimes in college—just to be cool," Elinor said.

Béatrice seemed to think this very funny and tossed her head back and giggled. She actually giggled flirtatiously, which annoyed Elinor. She watched Béatrice part her full lips, as if in slow motion, and show her large even teeth, stained from tobacco. She saw all her gold and silver capped molars and dental work. In her own privileged life, Elinor's teeth were flawlessly white, her perfect smile had been straightened by braces when she was a teenager. None of these defects had any effect on her attraction to Béatrice, however. In fact, Elinor was conscious of taking a luxurious pleasure in her nearness. Up close, the lines of her face seemed only to amplify her beauty, experience and age. She had four children. All of this placed her in some marvelous, unlikely category. That they should share much of the same drudgery and situation in life amazed Elinor. That they could be so much alike and yet so different. Elinor knew there were days Béatrice stood leaning against the kitchen counter as she did, smoking perhaps, or drinking a glass of wine to calm her nerves. Elinor noticed the same crease of annoyance form between Béatrice's brows that she had. She recognized her impatience with her children, like when Antoine had whined of a stomachache, ruining her plans to work out. Elinor certainly had the same impatience, particularly with Alexi who never seemed to be able to please her mommy as Clara did, which Elinor recognized as the worst thing that could happen to a child. Would it make her grow up to despise her, hate her as a sullen teenager for all she had done to her? It had made Alexi so angry that she cut off all her hair. Elinor suddenly told the story to Béatrice.

Alexi had been playing upstairs, very quietly it seemed for hours on her own. Suddenly she came running down the stairs and threw herself onto Elinor's lap.

"I . . . I . . . I cut all my hair off!" she screamed, trying to cover her head with her hands. "It's so awful!" she wailed in agony. "It's so awful and I'm so, so, sorry!" There she stood, looking like Anne Frank from the concentration camp—skinny, miserable and waifish with her hair in patches. At first, Elinor was so shocked, she didn't know what to do. Then she took Alexi in her arms and told her it was okay, trying not to laugh herself, of course, to relieve her own pain, knowing that Alexi would have to go to school like that and feel the shame for what she had done if the other children laughed at her. Elinor had soothed her, whispering, "You're not taking the easy way, are you Alexi?"

Elinor told Alexi it was cool and that she looked just like Anne Frank who was a famous writer when she was just a little kid just like her and that people who always behaved themselves and never took the hard way, or experimented, never turned out to be very interesting. Elinor was secretly proud of her for being such a wacky little kid, always insisting to go her own way, despite anything Elinor did or said. She knew it must be terribly hard to have a perfectly graceful little sister whose behavior Elinor began to grow suspicious of, as if she were purposely choosing to be so angelic as a way of tormenting Alexi.

Béatrice listened sympathetically and laughed at her narrative, saying that her oldest was exactly the same—jealous of her younger sister. Her middle child, it was true, was charming, startlingly beautiful like a little model, so finely featured with willowy long limbs and a small childish frown that creased her perfect brow with perplexed intensity.

Their conversation was interrupted when the gate opened and their children, especially Alexi, hurled herself at Elinor.

"Mommy look at this fantastic book!" she fairly yelled at her. It was a religious book of prayer from the school that she had been allowed to take home. It had old-fashioned looking engravings of Mary and Jesus, telling his stories to children. Alexi knew Elinor must like it as she liked her religious statues and unusual art that decorated their house. Elinor did like it, and she loved how much Alexi liked it. She was struck that a little kid, with all the children's books in the school library, should choose this one. Elinor said good-bye to Béatrice and lead Alexi and Clara to the car.

13

They began to meet like teenagers after dropping off their children at school and then went for coffee at the café on Place DeLille to talk, telling each other their lives. At length, tragic Béatrice revealed that she loved the *English Patient,* a film Elinor abhorred. It didn't surprise her, and she didn't care, Elinor still loved her. It was simply Béatrice's romantic sensibilities and Latin blood, something entirely out of her control and that she couldn't possibly help. Béatrice told Elinor that she secretly rode her husband's motorcycle around town to *reprend* her *jeunesse* (take back her youth). She taught Elinor to *fait un canard,* do a duck—to place the sugar cube in the coffee spoon and then dunk it in her café, careful not to let it sweeten the coffee and watch it soak up the café for a moment and then slurp it off the spoon, sweet like candy, to go with the bitter thick drink.

Sitting at the café, side by side, facing the street under the *parapluie,* Béatrice took off her sunglasses to show Elinor her red-rimmed eyes.

"I couldn't sleep at all last night. I kept waking up, and then I couldn't get back to sleep." she said pleadingly. Elinor searched her face. "Something's happened. I can't explain it, but things are not the same since . . . I came back to France."

Elinor waited with interest. Would she tell her something? Would she explain in words what she felt? But she was distracted. Elinor watched as the group of American ladies came up to the café from the school. They saw the two of them and avoided them. Grace, feeling the necessity of an explanation said, "We're just going to sit over here, okay?" Elinor was anxious but relieved.

"Okay," she said, although there were certainly plenty of tables nearby. She knew by now that language is a very real barrier and *does* separate people. She didn't insist they join them, although they were curious about the two of them sitting together. Elinor felt their interest, but she felt their contempt as well. It was true, their tête-à-tête forbade intrusion. Béatrice had a rather exclusive personality once she considered Elinor her friend. Elinor noticed she preferred to wait for her at her van rather than near the gate. Elinor's other friends came up to chat, but they didn't stay for long. Béatrice was unresponsive, as if indignant that they should trample the delicate bloom of their friendship with their audacious English.

"I've been married to Luc for eleven years," she continued in a weary tone. "Men are incredibly selfish. I'm sure it's their mothers' fault for taking such good care of them, loving them so unconditionally when the fact is—what's so great about them? They always think they deserve more, that we don't fulfill their needs. I'm tired of it. He keeps thinking there's always something better somewhere else all the time. *C'est pas vrai* and he's always disappointed. He doesn't like to be tied down, even to a job. He's unreliable and has quit his job before just because he was bored. We had to live off social security. But with four children, one cannot be so selfish," she said bitterly. "It's not good for the children to never stay in the same place for any length of time or form attachments."

Elinor listened.

"I live temporarily, always ready to be told we're leaving. That we have to move. We're never settled. I can't keep doing this to my kids." But Elinor knew she meant, 'I can't keep doing this to myself.' Béatrice smiled her melancholic smile and laughed, as if to reassure herself that it didn't matter—she was used to it.

"*C'est pas drôle,*" she said, watching the people walk by in front of the café. "I could move to my mother's. I've done it before."

"You can't do that," Elinor said, but it came out sounding hopeful and in the same moment, she knew that of course she should stay with her husband. Béatrice's manner changed, almost as if she had read her thoughts.

"I suppose, if one stays settled, one is in danger of becoming bourgeois." Béatrice smiled sadly and laughed. "It keeps me from being bourgeois."

Elinor was struck by the fact that Béatrice would wish to prevent such a fate, considering everyone she knew, her American girlfriends, were all trying so hard to be just so—*bourgeois*. Elinor would go back to her own bourgeois life in the States of enormous automobiles and decorating a house. But wasn't that the way to get over it? Get over her? Picking out colors and tile, a rest in the country would dull the senses enough when nothing could replicate the ecstasy of what she was feeling.

Elinor toyed with the packet of sugar cubes on the saucer of her petit café and looked around at the people at the other tables. She could not get over her situation, sitting at a French café, speaking French and fitting in so marvelously well, anyone would have thought she was French. Could Hemingway boast of this, she considered, in his expatriate years in Paris? Could Johnny Depp? Béatrice sat before her—lovely, married to Luc, the wild looking professor. She had a great talent for being beautiful and tragic, and when she told Elinor that she married him at twenty because she was pregnant, it seemed to perfectly unite the consequence of beauty with tragedy. Béatrice had had no ordinary life as Elinor had and she said she did it for all the usual reasons—a hatred of home, lust for the man she was to marry and the wish to be taken away from it all, never dreaming that she would be taken away—to Africa. For when Elinor considered it, she understood it all as Béatrice described it to her as the perfect prison, constructed of a useless husband and many children. She would never have any peace. Never sit as she liked, quietly in the sun and think. There would always be someone to please.

"But I was in love with him once. *C'était un vrai coup de foudre*, like a clap of thunder. Have you never been in love?" she asked, taking a cigarette from the pack of Gitanes and setting it on the café table. Elinor thought of her first trip to Paris almost twenty years ago.

"Perhaps not," Elinor said. *Except with you*, she left out, feeling at once ashamed for her childish crush. She momentarily looked past Béatrice to the table of American women when she heard Deborah say, ". . . and I said, if you want to have sex in the next century, you need to take off that ridiculous black bikini and put on a brief like a normal guy!" Everyone was laughing, and Elinor stared at them in awe for having such a good time. It seemed quite wonderful really. She watched their mouths, red with lipstick, and their colored hair, and she was distracted enough to consider how they looked, doing what indeed should be done at a café— enjoying themselves—and she knew suddenly how that might appear to the French—ridiculous, of course. How in the world could one carry on, having such fun when women in Afghanistan were being wrapped up in sack cloth and transported like so much crated cargo in the back of a scooter jalopy? While war threatened Iraq? Wasn't that the fundamental difference between the French and the Americans, Elinor thought. The French were essentially pessimistic and Americans optimistic.

She suddenly had a great desire to say something funny, or laugh hysterically, stand up with her hands on her hips like Robin Williams's version of La Quinta Chablis and say, "Listen child, you don't have to dress like a beekeeper girlfriend, you just tell your man, *uh-uh*." But exaggeration and humor seemed to never be taken for anything but madness or the truth. And it seemed impossible to translate anyway and even if she succeeded, Béatrice was certain to stare at her dumbfounded, wondering what effect she was going for and thoroughly confused as to what should be her reaction.

"No, it was different for me," Elinor said quickly, "I was twenty-six and too old to fancy myself in love." She meant it as a joke. Béatrice leaned back in her chair and studied her, taking a deep contemplative drag on the cigarette. Elinor watched her elegant hands and long, finely boned fingers take the cigarette from her mouth. "Béatrice, love is a commodity that women exchange to secure themselves in life, and marriage always compromises love."

Béatrice looked at her with amazement for her decidedly unromantic viewpoint, and for a moment Elinor was sorry she had said it. But it was simply that she would have never dreamed Béatrice could be as unfortunate as she was lovely. That her beauty, in her youth, was perhaps the very cause of her misfortunes. Falling in love when one is much too young to have the sense to choose someone who can be of use to them always ends in discontent. It is inevitable that children conceived in these lusty affairs will always find themselves to be a great inconvenience to their mother after her youth and chances are gone. Béatrice was convinced that her value was contained in her beauty and that even Elinor might soon discover the truth about her—that there was nothing beyond her looks. Béatrice's beauty, it occurred to her, had never been any great advantage to herself, rather it was perhaps her greatest liability.

"Yes, but how can you be satisfied with your life?" Béatrice ventured, curiously.

"Everyone imagines that everybody else is more at peace with themselves, that their lives must be more satisfying and complete. While at the same time they try so persistently to prove that theirs is certainly the best. It's exhausting. Béatrice, I have a handsome husband and beautiful children as you do, but don't imagine that makes me perfectly satisfied. I am as capricious as a child, and the only way I remain faithful and responsible is by lowering my expectations considerably." Whatever. It seemed so hard to really explain herself to Béatrice in French. It seemed easier to listen to her and try to understand *her*.

"Do you love Victor?" Béatrice asked with intensity, her eyes searching her face.

"Yes, I do," Elinor said, looking away from her. It was the truth. Couldn't she love Victor and Béatrice at the same time? "But husbands are tiresome enough. And husbands without jobs are even worse."

She did love Victor, because he was so good. But she knew she did not feel the same passion for him as she felt for Béatrice. Her love for Béatrice was entirely romantic, removed from marriage, family and responsibility.

It was contained in her admiration of her, the fact that they were so much alike and that to love her was impossible, but yet she trembled in the anticipation of it every moment they were together.

Béatrice seemed surprised and disappointed by her answer. She seemed so confident that Elinor loved her, although nothing had ever been said, it was always implied in their relationship that could never be considered common. It was true that Elinor did love her, but she would never say it. She was too afraid of her. Elinor knew why she loved Victor and was always so certain of his love. Of course she had known vaguely before that she detested self-satisfaction and he was the first person she had ever met who she could discover no such thing in. But suddenly, she knew precisely why she loved him and that their marriage would always be good. It was because Victor, unlike any other person—most particularly, man—she knew, couldn't imagine that it could get any better than this, that it could be any better with someone else and everyone always imagines that it must be better than this and that they must be happier with someone else. Because Victor's love, his goodness, was not ridiculous as many would contend. But Elinor didn't tell her this. She didn't want to spoil it, hurt her feelings, seeming perfectly content in her life while clearly Béatrice was questioning everything in hers. Their relationship was indeed romantic, and the fact that they were in love with each other was apparent, but it was the extraordinary circumstances of their friendship that made them in love. Elinor was not prepared to sacrifice everything important and dear to her, leave what was conventional in her life for a possible exquisite unknown. It was too frightening. Elinor watched her American friends get up and leave the café.

When they were gone, Béatrice reached out and touched Elinor's ear, under the pretense of admiring her earring, *"Elles sont ravissantes.* Where did you get them?" she asked and slid her fingers behind Elinor's ear and caressed the earlobe with her thumb for several moments.

Victor had given them to her, but she said instead, "I don't remember, I've had them forever." She sat very still, under her caress. At that moment, her girls were laughing and shouting, locked in tight behind the iron gates in the courtyard of the school, oblivious to the disruption of the earth. Don't whisper it, don't say it. Don't say that you love her and that you cannot have her because of the absurd circumstances of sex and civilization, because of the vast differences and similarities between you.

"You are so fine—*tellement belle,*" Béatrice whispered. Elinor was thrilled. Like a childish wish, more than anything in the world, she wanted to admire her, too, whisper how beautiful she was. Elinor felt crippled and dumb. Her singular method of making sense of the world, her natural talent for expressing herself was stolen away by living as a foreigner in France, making it impossible to express herself in any other way than to reach for this woman and embrace her full on the mouth, transmit the message that had existed without words in either language. Not as a man kisses a woman, but as a woman kisses a man, with a wanton directness that was unmistakable. But even as she became aware of these feelings, she was paralyzed by the perversity of them—repelled by the strength of her desire so that she appeared just as she felt, helpless and vulnerable and slightly contemptuous of Béatrice's advantage. After all, it was Elinor who loved her and Béatrice who had provoked her. But it was Béatrice who leaned forward and placed her lips lightly on Elinor's, watching her as she did so, and kissed her good-bye as naturally, as if it were the French *bisou* between girlfriends. Elinor, awed by her courage, closed her eyes, afraid to move, and kissed her back, so that they both knew what they meant by it. That yes, Elinor thought, it is like that. I do love you like *that.*

It happened so quickly that Elinor, for a moment, thought she might have imagined it. Béatrice stood to go.

"*Merci, pour le café,*" she said and went away.

Part II
Freedom Kiss

14

The war in Iraq started, and Elinor had been avoiding the appalling reality of it during the weeks that precipitated it. Certainly there was everything that led up to it and Elinor's shock that the French and the Americans should become rivals instead of allies. She felt so inadequate to explain, as she certainly must, herself, and her country. To ignore it was impossible. She, so shocked by the turn of the events, watched it play out on the television. It seemed such an audacious example of American arrogance, imperialism even, that was so contemptible to the French, such a perfect demonstration of what she was sure the French knew Americans to be anyway, what she herself had witnessed so often as she lived as an American in France, that she was mortified, ashamed and cruelly disappointed. But at the same time, her feelings were very much like a child's loyalty to a sister, with whom she has just been bitterly teasing, calling names, and pushing to the ground—the minute the other children joined in the taunting, she was ready to defend her with everything she had.

For the French would watch every day America exerting its will on the world and forcing it to conform to what it knew was best for everyone. Didn't everyone know they were the best, most powerful country in the world and shouldn't everyone else follow their example? She was afraid she would watch America get even stronger, while everyone else got smaller. It was too much for her to bear, even if perhaps for wholly selfish reasons.

Now everyone was so cautious and well behaved. The American ladies left the playground in the morning after dropping their children without saying hardly a thing, but a few quick greetings. Americans are united by optimism and their refusal to believe that there is any danger or trouble in the world, although strict security measures were put in place at the school. They dropped off their children, hoping to demonstrate to them their confidence that everything was fine, safe and secure.

Harriet Randall looked especially wounded and bewildered, and Stephanie Jacob particularly could be seen on the courtyard of the school visibly perturbed, with a bizarre light burning in her eyes. The day had come, she knew. Every event confirmed it. At last it was Judgment Day that she had anticipated and would now be witness to. Stephanie had prepared herself, however, and was ready to claim her fate and have her salvation confirmed while others burned in hell. Now the Rapture would begin and the nonbelievers would learn their folly, and know her as one of His chosen servants, know that she and Brad had always been good, clean and respectable. She would not be overlooked, her tidy virtues and well-regulated desires were unmistakable among the great filthy mass of sin that afflicted the rest of humanity. She would hardly share her place in paradise with trash, Arabs, Catholics and lunatics who mostly sat on the floor and ate with their hands. They certainly looked rather dangerous on the television, dancing, clapping and leaping like frogs.

Elinor saw Béatrice at the supermarket and was suddenly afraid of her. Elinor spotted her in produce wearing a blue and green scarf before she saw her. It was hard to miss her among all the other dreary customers picking over the fruits and vegetables, fervent as rodents, sniffing and squeezing and greedily filling their baskets. Elinor was at once afraid to meet her and then desperate to. She tried to ignore her and made for the cheese aisle, staring down at her hands gripping the cart. She felt wholly unprepared to deal with Béatrice's romantic beauty just then. She had Clara with her and was not feeling particularly glamorous, wearing one of Victor's insulated work shirts and a pair of blue jeans. She lacked Béatrice's wonderful French elegance that could dress up something equally drab with a colorful scarf. Elinor hurried past but felt Béatrice follow her out of produce. She turned down another aisle, never looking back.

"Mommy," Clara said, "remember when we saw ladies and gentlemen smoking cigarettes like this?" She held up her two extended fingers, holding an imaginary cigarette between them. Then she took her fingers away from her red puckered mouth and blew her a kiss.

She must settle what differences now existed between them, Elinor thought. Plead innocence, her case against the United States and George Bush, so that Béatrice could be sure, never suspect that she approved of such reckless, audacious behavior. Her limits in the language frustrated her, and she longed to express herself openly and easily without effort. Feeling silly, inarticulate, and clumsy exhausted her. The French seemed to communicate through some mysterious vagueness that didn't require words, anyway. In fact it was as if putting something to words might diminish its depth of meaning. This was in striking contrast to her own mad desire to express *everything* in words. Elinor suddenly felt entirely helpless in her situation.

She wished to escape, and she turned toward yogurt. Dairy took up nearly four separate aisles to accommodate over two hundred and fifty different kinds of cheeses, but when she turned the corner, they ran into each other. Elinor watched Béatrice hesitate, perhaps wanting to flee herself, and then they acknowledged each other. Elinor forced herself to smile and pretend she was pleasantly surprised to see her, but then felt suddenly ashamed as if she had sought her out.

They stood awkwardly, resolved not to kiss when a kiss was truly required. The French kisses on each cheek express their affection without having to say anything. It is particularly necessary in awkward moments between friends who wish to communicate their warmth while avoiding an awkward moment of what to say. Béatrice had the twins with her, and Elinor said how nice it must be to have so much help.

"C'est bien d 'avoir beaucoup d 'aide comme ça," she said, smiling at little Elisabeth who was fussing in the front of the cart. Neither Clara nor Elisabeth would cooperate very much by acknowledging each other or saying "bonjour" as both the women insisted, a bit too persistently, they do. Béatrice looked very uncomfortable and seemed as eager to leave as she was to see Elinor.

"It's terrible, what's happened," Elinor began to say. "I really cannot understand it, and don't know what to think myself."

"Yes, it is," she agreed and then was silent.

"You know, I am shocked," Elinor persisted. "I'm not sure they know what they're doing. It certainly is unprecedented. I mean they certainly are not very equally matched," she said and then was ashamed. She knew her words were entirely inadequate, but nothing she could say in French seemed to articulate her feelings. They stood awkwardly without saying a word. Because Béatrice was obviously more skilled in the language, Elinor often thought she ought to carry the burden of these types of awkward moments, but now it was Elinor who insisted she make herself perfectly clear, although she struggled to do so. "I, I do not agree with it," she said weakly.

"It is shocking indeed and certain to be a disaster for everyone. I'm sure it's horrifying to see your soldiers killed or taken as prisoners. But I don't see what they expect. The Americans always act in their own interest without any attention to how it might affect other countries, and they certainly have proved that they need not consult anyone or ask for any approval. It seems that they'll act ruthlessly, regardless. I cannot see that it will solve anything, but instead it will leave destruction and ruin as every other war has done."

Oh *God*, it was brutal. Béatrice's predictable reply was, Elinor could not help feel with a kind of disgust, *so French*. Everything was always certain to be a catastrophe. How could she, an American, possibly be expected to understand the position of anyone but herself?

Perhaps it was the public place, the surprise of their meeting. Perhaps

Béatrice had been waiting to say this. But Elinor just stood and stared. She really had no arguments to plead in French. She suddenly felt herself about to cry and then afraid to. Every night she listened to the French television prove that the war was and would certainly be a disaster as if it were shouting at her in an "I hate to say I told you so" fashion, "but that is why they are *them* and we are *we*." It was as if someone were shaking her and shouting, "Are you blind, what were you thinking? Don't you see Americans will gobble up the world and leave nothing for the rest of us."

It seemed immediately apparent that they never really knew each other at all and never would. Elinor suddenly wished more than anything to flee, to run away from the foreigness of her situation. If she thought the event of the war would separate her from Béatrice, she would never recover, and she knew their stay in France was over anyway. She and Victor had already discussed it. His job in France was up. They would be moving back to the States at the end of the school year, and Elinor was at once elated and devastated. The turn of events simply made her more desperate to go.

Their differences were so distinct, it seemed impossible to know one another now. It was horribly painful, like a slap in the face, and Elinor felt herself recoil physically. She was an overconfident suitor, shocked that his advances were unwanted and thus rejected. She suddenly felt a desperate failure—a failure to not have said something brave or noble, stand up for her country even, but instead she was struck dumb by the overwhelming helplessness in the face of a silent hostility she felt everywhere around her and a bitter regret that she hadn't noticed it before. Their relationship so delicately balanced between love and hate, even on her part, relied so much on her explanation. Her voice shook when she said, *"I'm sorry."*

"It's not your fault, *bien sur*," Béatrice said, and reached out to place her hand lightly against Elinor's shoulder. Embarrassed and uncomfortable in the public place of the supermarket, Elinor knew that they both wished desperately to leave. She stepped away from Béatrice's touch.

"I'll call you," she said, and they parted.

They had to carefully avoid each other while they completed the rest of their shopping. It was brutal, and the whole episode made Elinor ache to somehow explain—her inarticulateness was agony. What was this between them that was every day implied but never expressed? This intense curiosity to know one another, yet the agonizing reluctance to express it, except in a physical way. It made her feel profoundly foreign, and she could not comprehend it. And the war, it occupied her everyday, watching it play out eerily like a science fiction movie, listening to the French on the television condemn it as a failure, determined to prove it a disaster, *"les Americains, les Americains,"* she heard over and over till she would go mad. It confirmed that it was inevitable she must leave. She felt herself an unwelcome, boorish guest.

She went back to produce, which she had skipped, and where she knew Béatrice had already gone, so there was no chance of running into her again. She was looking over the fruit, occupying herself with a grape, as if deciding what to do next. She put it in her mouth and began to chew.

"I saw that."

Elinor turned around, startled after her unnerving encounter with Béatrice. It was Brad Jacob grinning at her with a boyish joy, an odd look of satisfaction on his face.

"Oh, that," she said rather relieved it was only him, "the grape?" It was rather startling to be approached so unexpectedly in English in produce at the supermarket, although perhaps not unusual, as nearly everyone in the whole city shopped there. He was standing in plastic sports sandals and shorts, but his somewhat obscene state of undress in the early spring, like some unpeeled fruit exposed to bruising, had no effect on his confidence. He was entirely pleased with himself and in finding her *par hasard* in the supermarket. He swooped in for the French kisses on each cheek. She kissed him back as graciously as possible, although it depressed her to do so. They were compatriots, however, and were connected by their shared circumstances. They both knew that the kiss sealed their solidarity, and she would never escape the familiarity now. Stephanie would hate her, and their relationship would be strained. And why not? Kissing had never been an American custom, and she wasn't sure it was a French custom either in the supermarket, between two people who barely knew each other. She had refused even to kiss Béatrice.

"Are they any good?" he asked quizzically, and she looked down to watch him caress one of the large black grapes between his fingers.

"You're asking me if grapes are any good in France?" she said with a little more sarcasm than she intended. He laughed.

"Well, as often as I drink them, I rarely eat them."

"Oh?" she said, because although she didn't know Brad Jacob very well other than having shared a table for dinner at Christmas, she had heard a great deal of him from the ladies at coffee. He often made it his duty to give the blessing before dinner gatherings, and she knew from living in the South that indulgence in alcoholic beverages was to be done with the strictest caution and moderation. Enjoyment of fine wine, particularly, was hedonistic in nature, because it implied consuming it for pleasure, not only for its dangerous effects. She could not help but feel that Stephanie's enthusiasm to introduce Bible study, for instance, and his own condescension to exist good naturedly among people he considered decidedly beneath himself, was an effort to exert some influence over the community, to set a moral example over such potentially wicked engagements as cocktail and dinner parties where the conversation often tended toward the suggestive or flirtatious sort of teasing that went on between married people. She often noticed a hush or a guarded self-consciousness, and a great many uncomfortable silences develop among her normally easygoing friends when one of the Jacobs entered into the conversation.

The Jacobs' self-importance was something awesome and powerful. One must be careful, Deborah had warned, what one says in the presence of the Jacobs. "They are *very* religious, you know."

And now he stood before her, handsome and charming, assuming an intimacy she did not feel or desire, determined to prove he was nothing at all like what she suspected.

"Then you're enjoying the fine wine in France?" she asked skeptically, dropping the bunch of grapes in a bag to prove she would buy what she had sampled. They were avoiding the topic of war, perhaps convinced that they should disagree on the issue completely. Elinor couldn't help feeling offended by his presence, watching her put the grapes in the bag, though it was friendly enough. Perhaps it was simply her encounter with

Béatrice that had upset her nerves and made her annoyed. He reached across her to get a bunch of the dripping grapes himself, giving her a rakish glance, as if she was supposed to swoon or something over the suggestive gesture.

"Yes, I've been collecting on our trips," he said, his face large and close. It was like he had never gotten over himself since high school when, she might admit, he probably did make all the girls swoon and this self-assurance made her think him particularly a fool and a boor. "The house has a *cave*, you know," he continued, and she couldn't help noticing the fact that he had said *the* house, as if it were famous, or something.

"*Ah*. A *cave*. And how do you like *the* house?" she asked.

"It's great! You will have to come out and see it sometime."

"I'd like that," she said politely.

"Steve Hannig was in town just a few weeks ago for meetings and was over to the house for dinner. He said he knew you from home."

"Yes, we lived in the same building."

"We talked about you."

"Oh?" she said. She barely knew this Steve Hannig person. Although she knew he was rather highly placed in the company and was surely a welcome guest at the Jacobs for dinner, she could not really claim him as anything more than a brief acquaintance from the apartment complex. What could he possibly have to say about her? Elinor knew of him simply by association with her husband's job, and she was always wearied by discussions that tended toward who one knew or had to dinner. "I'm sorry I wasn't there to defend myself."

"He said he used to run into you at the pool," he said raising his eyebrows meaningfully, although she remembered nothing of such encounters.

"*Did he?*"

"I bet you looked good."

"*Uh-huh*. And what did *he* think of the house?" she said to change the subject. He seemed so determined to be cheerful and avoid any discussion of the war. But it was this insistence to avoid the topic that confirmed his views.

"Very French. It is you know, the kids love it. It's interesting to explore, and the living room has a rococo frieze all the way around. It's beautiful," he said, as if this might please her and convey that he understood something about it as art. "I mean, perhaps it is a little much for us, but I just thought, when will we ever get a chance to do something like this again? And a good portion of it has been redone. It has a new kitchen, laundry room and bathrooms. Stephanie doesn't like it," he said suddenly. "She doesn't like anything. I don't know how to make her happy." He said it miserably with his eyes downcast, and then he slowly raised them to hers, inviting her into his confidence, imagining that she must be sympathetic, sharing his complaint that she should never be privy to. Stephanie, who could only bear the unpleasantness of life with the greatest forbearance and thorough disappointment was, Elinor conceded, perhaps a rather dreary companion. But Elinor pretended not to notice, even though suddenly the fruits and vegetables seemed silent witness to their conversation.

"You were very active in your church, I think, and I know that Stephanie misses that a lot. Perhaps it is just a matter of time. It's always difficult to adjust to the differences in the way of life here in France. And when you have lived in the States with every possible privilege, luxury and convenience at your disposal, it's difficult to adjust to even the slightest deficiency." He stood staring, not knowing what to make of her. "But when the adjustment is accomplished, it's nearly impossible not to be very shocked—even outraged, by the kind of extravagance considered indispensable in the States. Life is so simple and beautiful here, and my advice is to enjoy it as much as you can. Because you're right, when will we ever do this again?" she said, yanking another grape off its stem and popping it in her mouth.

"You're right," he said. Elinor believed she had sufficiently discouraged him. "That's why I'm out here on a Friday. Stephanie sent me out for charcoal and *grillades* to get the weekend started early. I'm sure she never thought I'd have the chance to meet you."

Elinor felt suddenly awkward and desperate to get away.

"Well," she said. "It sure is nice not to spend all the warm weather away, taking care of the yard like at home."

"Yes it is," he agreed. She told him to have a good weekend, grabbed the handle of her cart and said good-bye, steering it away toward the bell peppers, large and uncommonly bright in color. They were like *l'objets d 'art*. Elinor thought she could feel his notice as she picked one out, pretending to evaluate its goodness. There were enough people in produce for them to lose each other gracefully. Elinor ran her thumb over the waxy skin of the vegetable, keeping her eyes fixed there, waiting as if she were feeling for a pulse, something that would tell her that this was the one. She hardly ever put bell peppers in anything. What was she going to do, make fajitas, she thought chaotically, as she bagged the pepper and moved in the direction she felt sure he had not gone in.

15

She and Victor woke at the crow of the cock quite literally and drove with the children out of their medieval village toward Bordeaux. The announcement that *les Americans* had destroyed an Iraqi marketplace on the car radio seemed such a startling contrast to the ancient countryside that Elinor turned it off, and they drove in silence. They were on their way to Bordeaux and then Madrid to escape for the spring holiday. There was very little *autoroute* on the way to Bordeaux from Cherbourg, so they were forced to drive through Dordogne, perhaps the most beautiful region in all of France. It is the land Henry Miller described as *a land of enchantment, jealously marked by poets and which they alone have the right to call their own. Which is closest to heaven . . . Nothing will stop me believing that this great, peaceful region of France is destined to remain a sacred place for man and that, when the big city has finished wiping out poets, their successors will find refuge and a birthplace here. For me, this visit to Dordogne was of capital importance—I still have hope for the future of mankind and even our planet. It is possible that one day France will cease to be, but Perigord will survive like the dreams which nourish the human soul.*

They stopped first at a fascinating site that caught their eye on the roadside. Saint Angel was the name of the village with the imposing site of what was called an *eglise fortifie*, or fortified church, perched high on the hillside. Saint Angel looked deserted at that hour of the morning— ten o'clock, nothing was stirring. Despite the rather damp weather, they stopped and got out to investigate, careful to avoid the snails that had, in large numbers, appeared to absorb the morning moisture that still clung to the grass. The children were thrilled and collected a few. There seemed to be hundreds of varieties and colors with different types of shells—one that was enormous who they called *le grandpère*. They picked the wild strawberries that grew along the wall, and the children were delighted to taste them. They were tiny and sweet.

"It's a little magical!" Clara said with enthusiasm. Elinor agreed, it did seem a little magical. The strange and enormous population of snails seemed to be the only residents in the silent village of Saint Angel and the red berries that grew sweet in April as if enchanted by some marvelous spell.

It was about ten degrees colder inside the church, although it was the end of April, and their breath rose like ghosts and disappeared up into the chilly air. The great door echoed shut in the silent empty church devoted to Saint Michel the Archangel, slayer of the dragon. There was a magnificent statue of him at the apse, in full armor and raised sword. He stood above the reptilian demon, with his great wings spread. He was beautiful, frozen in the act of slaying the demon with a pure expression of his holy purpose painted on his smooth angular face. Elinor suddenly thought she would like to steal him. She suddenly wanted to lift him down from his pedestal and throw him in the back of the minivan and drive away. No one would know or probably even care. He might never even be noticed as missing. She was suddenly thoroughly ashamed of herself. I have the heart of a thief, she thought miserably and said nothing to Victor, but turned and left, silently shutting the heavy door behind them.

They drove for nearly an hour in silence, and the children fell asleep.

"There is a woman at the school," Elinor began. "It's very strange. I met her. I saw her near the beginning of the school year." It was suddenly incredible that all this time, with all the turmoil of her feelings, she had never mentioned Béatrice to Victor. "It's rather silly really, but I feel like I'm cheating on you," she laughed. Victor listened patiently.

"I was struck by her at the beginning of the school year and well, we've gotten to be friends. And now we meet each other for coffee, and it's all very strange," she stopped.

"What? What's strange about that?"

"Well, it *is* strange. I mean *how* we meet, how we met."

"Is she French?"

"Yes. You see, she's very beautiful, and I noticed her the first time I saw her, and I think she noticed me, too, and then we kept on noticing each other in a way . . . that implied something. It's hard to explain."

"Well, it doesn't sound strange to me. I think it's great you made a French friend," he said proudly.

"No, it is strange," she said. "I'm trying to tell you why, why it's strange. Because it's a bit like, well, it's like I fell in love with her." Victor turned away from the road and looked at her.

"What're you talking about?" he laughed.

"That I fell in love with her, that I fell in love with a woman and that we meet each other for coffee."

"What're you talking about Elinor, are you telling me you're having an affair with a woman? What? Are you sleeping with her?" he said excitedly.

"N-o-o-w-a," she sang out lightly as if that would be the most absurd thing in the world.

"Then what? So you meet each other for coffee?"

"Well, yes."

"And?"

"And, it's strange. That's all . . . because there's this kind of attraction between us. It's a kind of sexual attraction."

"Okay, so what're you trying to say?"

"That it's romantic, sexual even, and that I sort of . . . love her, am infatuated with her."

"And what, you want to run away together?" He was starting to enjoy the conversation, she could tell. He was handling it as lightly as if it were fascinating, designed to entertain him for the ride to Spain.

"No. But it's bothering me. I feel like I'm losing my mind. I think about it all the time, and I know it's absurd, but I can't deny it either."

"What? What can't you deny?"

"That I fell in love with her." She stopped, amazed that she could say it out loud to her husband. And then she started to cry. "Don't you see," she said sobbing, "She's so beautiful, if you could see her." But at this she thought she might be jealous. It was not women who fell in love with beautiful women, but men who were vulnerable in this way. "She has something about her, something very capable. I guess I never met another woman like that. I know it sounds foolish and vain, but it's true, and I can't help how I feel."

Her sobbing was making her look pathetic or hysterical, she knew, and she tried to pull herself together. "Look, I know it sounds crazy, and it's making me crazy, but I can't help what's happened."

"What's happened?" he laughed, glancing back quickly to check the kids, who were sound asleep. "It's not like you've kissed her, have you?"

"No," she lied solemnly.

"Then what?"

"Nothing, except I fell in love with a woman, if you can consider that normal!" she said in a restrained staccato through her tears. "Look, it's stupid, I know. Maybe I shouldn't have told you. It's a chick thing, like a girlish crush, that's all. I just want to go home. It's too humiliating. Just forget it." And she was silent.

"Look, I'm sure this has been stressful for you. But it is interesting, and I think it's great that you made a French friend. Just enjoy it. I don't see how it can be humiliating. It's actually a rare accomplishment, and you only have a few more months before we have to leave, anyway. Just take it easy."

She could tell, he was trying to handle this well, rationally and intelligently. If Victor said it was all right, it was.

"I know it's crazy, and I'm sure it's just part of my love/hate relationship with France. I mean, it's a little funny actually. I just want to laugh out loud that in the end, even after three years, do they finally just prove themselves to be the rude, selfish bastards we think of them as or is that part of their charm?" She laughed through her tears. "But in fact, the French are charming to no one. The entire culture has never been any-thing but tolerated by tourists and *etrangers*. I mean, it's easy to love France, but it's impossible to love the French. But, part of what makes this all so painful is that I tried so hard. Maybe I took it too seriously, and now we have to leave this and go back. It won't be easy, Victor. It has made such an impression on me."

She thought of the desolate heat of the South, how she hated it. When they found out they would go to France, she felt the whole wide world lay open to her, she thought of all the beautiful things she had seen before—the Doge's Palace in Piazza St. Marco, Pompeii, Trafalgar's Square, the Royal Palace in Monaco, the Sistine Chapel, the Sagrada Famillia. What on earth would she do? All she could do was think of the bleak hum of a window unit, like the little filter on the fish tank, and the fluorescent tube lighting at the Dollar Store in the Bi-Lo Shopping Plaza, and the meticulously landscaped suburban sprawl. The thought made her head swim, and she felt nauseous, as if she had just received a prison sentence. She could hear herself talk of her travels, sounding idiotic, of course, like the snobbish wealth she watched bargaining at the flea market at Vaunves. She always separated herself from the innocence of American tourists, knowing how to conduct herself in French, chatting with the other mothers on the courtyard of the school, about Pascal's hip surgery, the twins, Melanie's baccalaureate exam, and Aurelien's speech impediment. Standing in the corridor of the school after dropping off Clara with her teacher and watching Alexi's class file up the stairs—Sophie, Florien, Solenne, Adèle, Marceau, Roman, Inès, the sound of their names were like music. Their familiar faces flashed across her memory, and she was fascinated that she knew them. She was a fool, of course, because she was never French, and the idea of leaving was terrify-ing but to stay was insanity. To be quaint and adorable was humiliating enough, but did she have to endure being just plain idiotic? Everyone insisted she explain how it was that America had come to appoint them-selves ruler of the world, imposing their inferior cuisine, film and puritanism against everyone's will—making her opinion speak for an entire country was as absurd as it was tiresome and she began to refuse. She was beginning to be bored in a way in which she knew was utterly blasé, must she endure another holiday in Spain?

They reached Poblet by about six, a bit south of Barcelona, and they set out immediately to visit the monastery that would close by eight. The sun shone on the warm yellow stone although the wind blew as fierce as the Provençal *mistral*. They admired the majestic simplicity and then just after the grounds closed, sought the comfort of the hotel after an exhausting voyage. The hotel was an enormous chateau-like stucco construction, splendid and freezing, with cold tile floors and large apartments—far too grand for even the hot Spanish sun to warm. Inside the large rooms, the radiators were stone cold. It didn't bother her at first, and they had dinner in the grand freezing dining room—her plate of grilled fish was divine. But after passing the night huddled under the thin woolen blankets, listening to the howling winds and banging shutters, she was reluctant to leave the meager comfort of the light bedding and place her icy feet on the cold Spanish tile, not to mention shower in the freezing bathroom. The morning seemed decidedly colder than last evening had with what little heat had accumulated the previous day from the sun. Elinor told the children to stay under their blankets.

Victor called down to the desk. It was nearly nine, but no one picked up, for who, especially tourists, not to mention working people, should be up before ten? It seemed they were the only guests in the enormous hotel, possibly the only people. The staff would not make an appearance perhaps until a more reasonable hour. But like most European hotels—they are privately owned, and the owners lived in what she was sure were cozy apartments behind the desk.

They brought up a portable heater which they placed in the bathroom while Victor and she showered—the children stayed under their blankets, watching *The Powerpuff Girls*.

"*La Ciudad del Townsville,*" the almost identical voice announced in Spanish. Alexi and Clara were entranced, and it was no use to try and heat the entire room. They were sturdy and agreeable little travelers but eager as well for a hot cup of *chocolat* at breakfast. They warmed themselves with hot coffee and *chocolat* and filled their bellies with bread and jam in the smaller more cozy breakfast room of the hotel.

After the six-hour drive through desolate Aragon they reached the sunny warm Spain they sought in Madrid. Victor navigated through the crowded city with the maps from guide books in search of the hotel. As they crossed the Puerta del Sol, a young man ran up to the car and knocked on the window. It was Fernando, a young Spanish man from her French class back in Cherbourg. They kissed and expressed in French—the only language they had in common, their amazement at what an extraordinary coincidence that he had seen her from the street and the incredible chance of meeting each other in the same city—he wasn't even from Madrid, just visiting friends for the holiday!

Madrid was wonderful, stately and proud—especially festive during *Semana Santa*, the Easter week. They visited *El Rastro*, the famous flea market filled with stylish New Yorkers keen on making a bargain.

"I got him down to three hundred," she heard them whisper ecstatically to each other. There was every kind of thing spread out in the street for sale—boots without their mates, old Milton Bradley games, typewriters in need of repair, and old record players and record collections among La Granja glass, rococo furniture, obscure but marvelous paintings, and to her delight, religious statues. However, she found that they were much more valued in Spain, as the Spaniards maintained their religion with enthusiasm, much more than the French. This also made them more expensive and sought after. They were not like the bargains she could pick up in France. She found a wonderful statue of Saint Isidro and Victor bought him for her. She was certainly as capable of robbing the Spanish of their treasures as the New Yorkers.

Sitting at a café on the Plaza Mayor, she and Victor argued over the Spanish menu for something to eat, particularly what would be appropriate for the girls. When the Spanish waiter came to take their order he had a look that seemed to obviously say, "I pity you sir. She may be blond and blue-eyed, but I don't envy you one bit, being married to that bossy American woman. I wouldn't care if she looks like Sharon Stone." Elinor gave him a charming smile as if she had caught his message loud and clear and let Victor make their order.

They sat in the warm spring sun and sipped Coca-Colas from tiny glasses with about four delicate chunks of ice and watched the Plaza as if it were a grand stage filled with spectacles—*les saltimbanques*, clowns, jugglers, and every kind of gig one could invent to entertain and gather a few coins from the tourists.

Rather near them was a band composed of three young men, singing and playing the Gipsy Kings. One sat on a homemade drum made from a wooden box to keep the beat, another strummed and beat the guitar and the third clapped and sang, *Djobi, Djoba*. After their song was done, they passed around a simple clear glass ashtray to the people sitting at the café tables, and many waved them away like flies off their food.

Alexi and Clara finished their lunch, and Elinor sent them out to run and play on the Plaza. When the singer began the sultry *Viento del Arena*, a young girl, seemingly from the crowd, in her blue jeans and simple tank T-shirt came out and slowly began to sway her hips and wave her hands with the startling, almost primeval grace of some exquisite bird. Every eye from among the blasé tourists turned and was immediately captivated, almost as if they had been waiting, to come to Spain expressly to see such an exotic performance. The girl whirled and danced on the ancient pavement like some ghostly vision from the past, her lovely pale face passing before them for an instant when she turned her large black eyes on the spectators. The quick grace of her movements was fantastic enough to fix every eye upon her as if she would vanish in a moment. While dancing, as if she had done it all her young life, a tress of her wavy black hair got loose and fell in front of her face and now emphasized the mystery of her. The elusive flash of her radiant Andalusian features was inconceivable enough to make one contemplate the reality of it. Was she indeed so beautiful as that, to be out on the Plaza on a Sunday afternoon, dancing for coins in her modern day attire, they all wondered. Perhaps it was a dare, *un jeux?* Alexi and Clara stopped playing and sat back at the table to watch her. She was hypnotizing, even to the children. The band members could hardly keep their countenance or be expected to play their music correctly, they were so distracted. But the effect was nonetheless charming. Elinor watched her for several songs. The young girl was so beautiful she thought she might cry. The girl grew warm with the exercise and tied her hair back away from her face with a scarf, low on her forehead, like a real gypsy. When she stopped dancing, she took the ashtray to collect the money from the now large gathering of spectators, and they showered her with coins which she took back dutifully to the three young men. They handed her out a few coins, and she ran away, off the Plaza, only to return a few minutes later with a Pepsi to cool herself.

Elinor gave Alexi and Clara money to take to her and though Alexi particularly was shy, they both summoned their courage as if it might be marvelous to approach her.

"Here," she instructed Alexi, "give it to Esmeralda. Give it straight to the girl, don't give it to the men." But although they did just as she had told them, the girl turned from them and gave it directly to the men.

In the heat of the afternoon they rested in the cool of their hotel room, and Elinor watched the girls playing gypsy dancers waving one of their T-shirts from the suitcase around like a scarf and insisting she tie it into their hair. Elinor was amazed watching Alexi invent their adventures as they traveled around, performed in the street and camped along the way. They seemed to know that they must find food and drink with the pennies she gave them to put in the hotel ashtray that they placed on the floor and danced around.

Elinor let them alone and went into the other room where Victor was laying on the bed, watching television. She would give them some distance to enter and stay in the world they had invented. Britney Spears was playing on one of the music channels, dancing and singing one of her pop songs, wearing a red rubber Barbarella costume like Jane Fonda, and Elinor lay down next to Victor and stared.

"Britney Spears has a video and can probably fill a stadium of teenagers for one of her performance, and yet she is nothing to the Andalusian girl on the Plaza Mayor," she said aloud. Victor agreed.

When she came back into the other room, she found her girls lumped together like kittens, asleep on the sofa bed as if in their imagination it might have been a Madrid Metro station.

16

Béatrice waited for Elinor by her van the Monday afternoon after the spring holiday smoking a cigarette with her booted foot up on the running board. It flaunted her masculine self-sufficiency and assurance that made Elinor almost hate these demonstrations that she felt were designed for her. After she pulled up and got out of the car, they did not pretend not to notice each other, but stood before one another in an awkward moment before they kissed shyly. Was it only Elinor with her puritan Americanness who was unnerved by the kiss? She suspected Béatrice was making fun of her.

Elinor politely asked how she had spent her holiday.

"I visited my sister in Paris. It was wonderful to get away from Luc and the children for awhile. You know, I don't think I missed them at all," she laughed. "It is so delicious to be by oneself, you know."

Little Elisabeth ran out into the street. Elinor heroically caught her by the arm and pulled her back. Béatrice yanked her onto the curb and scolded her vehemently, while little Antoine put his hand into Elinor's. What was she doing, the impulsive little thing, Béatrice scolded.

"Do you want me to lock you in the car?" she threatened. A portion of this strange attraction had to do with how much they recognized their similarities. Elinor had seen Elisabeth tug on her mommy with the same desperation for attention that Clara, and more particularly Alexi had. What a strange longing and curiosity they had for one another, this wondering how the other lives. Her life is like mine, Elinor knew. Béatrice knew it, too. Elinor wished she could ignore this curiosity and avoid these brief encounters that they hoped chance would allow them, because both of them were afraid of taking the next step. This longing might never occur in any other situation but the one they shared. Their late thirties, their roughly ten years of marriage, their girlish capriciousness, their fading beauty, their youth nearly spent, the childishness of unfulfilled dreams, and the disappointments that they shared.

They said little more as they walked to the gate, except that the weather was fine and then they stood together, waiting for the gate to open, speechless for what seemed like a long moment. Somehow a depth of understanding had developed that made it difficult to put to words, although Elinor had a great desire to resolve this whole awkwardness with words. Perhaps it was the language that prevented them from speaking, but in a way, it seemed so much had been communicated between them over the course of the year in a look, a gesture, a smile, that conversation or a revelation of these feelings was hardly necessary.

She could feel the sweat accumulate and drip down her body under her summer sweater. The minutes passed, and then she heard herself say, almost in a whisper, "Béatrice?"

Béatrice turned and looked at her, so hopelessly beautiful, like a girl, just like Elisabeth. *"C'est difficile d'avoir une vraie conversation devant le portail—devant la porte."* It was the frankness of the simple sentence that she hoped contained everything she wanted to say, *"C'est difficile."*

"You're right," Béatrice said, *"Non, je sais,* you must come up to my apartment again soon, for coffee," she said.

"You know, I'm leaving. I'm moving back to the States."

Béatrice looked at her, not at first understanding what she was saying.

"We are moving back to the States at the end of the school year," she continued.

"What for? *Qu'est ce que tu veux dire?* What do you mean?"

"We are going back to the States. Victor has accepted to be moved there by the end of the month. *C'est normal que,* we have to go. We cannot stay in France forever." She did not mention the war. That she was relieved to escape. Béatrice stared at her in disbelief, her disappointment apparent on her face in the brilliant sunshine. How could she do such a thing, Béatrice wanted to know, move again after everyone had settled in so well, made friends, her children, settled at school, which for the French, who are not at all suited to moving about the country, picking up their lives and getting on with one another very well at all. Her look of shock and betrayal surprised Elinor, almost as if any show of her feelings before had been a charade that had not fully convinced Elinor, and now she proved herself wholly sincere. Elinor stood stunned in the glare, missing Béatrice already with a desolate loneliness.

"*C'est court,* I mean, it seems so short, such short notice. You can't mean it."

Elinor felt dizzy and wanted to suddenly give it up and walk away. A quick exit seemed preferable than to live in the hope of continuing something superficial contained in the brief encounters before the gate and on the playground when anything might upset it now. And Elinor wished to leave rather than prolong the agony of their doomed attraction.

"Well, it's not exactly short. We've lived here for three years," she tried to say lightly.

Elinor had thought they were so much alike but knew that things beyond their control would drive them apart, and it would be too painful to live through. If she left, she could treasure Béatrice in her memory forever. If she stayed, she would lose her eventually. No, she wished to escape. By and by she would recover. *But I must leave,* she thought.

Their children were gathered around them vying for attention. They both gathered them up and heard what it was they had to say. Béatrice looked at her and smiled sadly.

"I cannot stay. Don't you see? It's for my girls and me, I'm not

French." Elinor said, believing it was true. She had every reason to go, the greatest reason of all was to leave her. What Elinor knew she felt for her had the power to destroy her life, but she also knew that once she was home she would have to live through a little agony each day in the memory of her. Perhaps it would go away over the years or perhaps it would grow stronger as her youth disappeared, and more of her life would be taken up in remembering. Elinor could not help but feel that their discussion was drawing attention from the other women on the playground.

"*De toute façon,* come to my house tomorrow, for lunch," Elinor said hopefully.

"Yes, of course," Béatrice said, gathering up her children to go. Elinor watched her as she went, turning her magnificent back and walking out of the gate.

Elinor walked with her girls back to the car feeling utterly defeated. Béatrice was embarrassing her, ruining her happiness, making her uneasy. What had started as a kind of flirtation between two women instead began to tear her down and wreck her confidence. She was suddenly tired of the whole thing, tired of love and longing—it seemed an exhausting pursuit, much more pleasant to be *drôle* than dreary and in love. She knew it was not worth it, but could not give it up. How might she go through the day without the hope of seeing her? How might she take her children to school and pick them up without seeing Béatrice's crappy van waiting for her? How could she feel such an attachment to someone, some powerful connection based on no real intimacy of mind. It all existed as a fancy of their imaginations. But to be certain that Béatrice felt it, too, and to let it go, to forget it would break her heart and leave her devastated, make her search the faces in the crowd her whole life for Béatrice.

When she got home, she ran up to the bathroom and looked at her defeated expression in the bathroom mirror. Leaning on the sink, she watched the tears spring to her eyes. She wanted her, she knew, and felt she would run mad if she could not have her and yet denied even at that moment what she felt as unnatural and forbidden. She stared through the tears at the bottles and tubes in her cosmetic case on the counter and noticed how less of it was makeup and more of it was creams, lotions and other products to preserve her youth. Part of all this was some last grasping for romance and the excitement that goes along with being young and beautiful, intriguing, and desirable. The excitement—childish, girlish—of wanting a beautiful friend, she told herself. She had watched her own little Alexi cry in anguish for a friend she had chosen who would not play with her and who tormented her, as children do, by singing, gleefully, "you're not my friend anymore!" She would watch Alexi's pain with some great curiosity as if Alexi's childish innocence held some secret truth. "Molly will not play with me!" she would wail in agony. And the sought-after little Molly relished her power and desirability, as if playing with such a desperate child couldn't interest her at all.

Elinor needed to explain herself. She had invited Béatrice to her house for lunch, although such a scheme seemed wrought with danger.

17

Stephanie Jacob arrived to pick up her little boy after Elinor had taken him home for lunch and to play for the afternoon with Alexi. Elinor invited her in to sit and offered her a coffee.

"I don't drink coffee," she said with a kind of pain and regret, as if she were sorry to disappoint her.

"Oh," Elinor laughed, "I thought you said you didn't drink coffee."

Stephanie stared, "I don't."

The first thing they talked of was the bullfights because Elinor said, "Mathew has been telling me all about them."

"Oh?" she said, a little embarrassed.

"I told him he has to go to Spain to see one for himself. Alexi knows all about them. I told him he should be a toreador for Carnival, you know you can buy those costumes in all the shops in Spain."

Stephanie was wearing her pained expression and Elinor was, she admitted, trying to give her some enthusiasm for living in Europe. She had boys. Wouldn't that be exciting to take them to Spain, she encouraged. Mathew was apparently very impressed with the whole thing, which seemed natural for something so dramatic and exciting for a little boy his age. Something Elinor always encouraged in their exploration of Europe—anything that the girls found interesting, encouraging them to believe in magic, fairies, romantic heroes and giants. She remembered visiting a Norman castle on a tour, the guide describing in meticulous detail all of the horrors and intrigues that had occurred in each room, all in French, the children hardly paying any attention, the guide showing them the gutter that ran along the side of the ballroom where the nobles could take a discreet pee during the dance.

When they came to the kitchen, with an enormous chimney and bare wooden tables with racks at each end for the men to rest their bloodied swords for the time it took them to eat before they returned to battle, Clara looked about her with alarm. The ceiling was hung with treacherous wrought iron meat hooks, and she stared at them in awe.

"This is where they eat the little children, Mommy," Clara whispered as she gazed at the dreadful hooks. It was a statement, not a question, as if she knew a great giant like the giant in *Jack in the Beanstalk* lived there.

Elinor might have said, "Yes sweetie, it is." She was always telling them about the dungeon where they locked up all the thieves and witches. Or how Jeanne d'Arc, was a beautiful hero in armor who was beckoned by angels and made such a row among the English. They shouldn't have burnt her, but they did. Elinor threatened that if they did not behave themselves, she would leave them to sell flowers on the street with the other little beggars, and only their beauty could save them. They had seen puppet shows in Brugges performed by odd looking dwarves with a bellydancing marionette whose costume and hair pop off at the end to reveal underneath is a skinny little man with a tattoo—the puppet had been in drag the whole time. They had seen blind women begging for money, their eyelids sewn shut to hide the vacant place where their useless or diseased eyes had been.

At such sights, she hurried the children past—the illuminated skeletons in the catacombs, the blood in gilt vials or ribs and skulls housed in effigies of saints. But she always encouraged them to imagine the fascinating stories that went along with such garish culture as was sometimes unavoidable in their adventures.

Elinor had heard Alexi in the garden playing with Celine, the little neighbor girl, one day. She came running in the house.

"There was a fairy in our garden," she cried. "Mommy, it was real, I saw it!"

"Really?" she said. "What did she look like, what color was she?"

"She was all in white, Mommy she was all white, just like a butterfly in a white dress." Elinor was stunned by her enthusiasm, her perfect innocence and joy.

"Let me get my shoes. *Shhh*, don't frighten her away. Show me where she is," Elinor said with excitement, hastily putting on her shoes.

"She flew away," Alexi said disappointed. "But she was real, Mommy. Celine said there's no such thing as fairies, but I saw her, really I did!" Elinor suddenly felt a little bit sick when Alexi said that. She knew that just because they lived in France didn't stop other children and even grown-ups from spoiling all the fun—telling Alexi that fairies didn't exist or that it was really your parents who put the prize under your pillow at night when you lost a tooth, stuffed your Christmas stocking, where babies really came from, and that women had periods, and soon all the magic would disappear. Elinor remembered Lynette Moore, third grade know-it-all and Miss America at eight years old, telling her that women bled between their legs. Naturally, Elinor was horrified. And when she asked her mother if it was true, her mother didn't even hesitate "Of course not. You go and tell Lynette Moore she doesn't know what she's talking about."

"You tell Celine that she doesn't know what she's talking about, and just because *she's* never seen one before doesn't mean they don't exist," Elinor had instructed Alexi.

Elinor didn't say all this to Stephanie of course. She looked quite horror-struck at the idea of the bullfight, that Elinor had encouraged her son's enthusiasm. Stephanie was rather like a princess, Elinor thought. Although she wanted to be a noble one, she was unfortunately prevented by a distaste for disagreeable and nasty things. Elinor could tell that

Stephanie's dislike of her created a great moral conflict within her, which as much as she struggled, she could not overcome.

"I didn't even know they were watching it, and I certainly didn't know the fights were so violent. I let the kids go up to watch TV in the hotel room while we waited for our order in the restaurant downstairs. She had finally taken our order, and I knew it was going to be a good bit before the food arrived. Well, that was about all that was on television at the time and it seemed to interest the kids well enough, so I wasn't really paying much attention until I saw them stick the bull in the back with knives, and he was gushing with blood. It was horrible. I just turned it off. They would never get away with something like that in the States," she said in a little fit.

Elinor stared at her, a little surprised. What was she even talking about? "Of course we would never do something like that in the States. It has nothing to do with our culture or tradition not to mention the animal activists . . ."

"I just never knew it was so violent. All I could think was how it's so much like the Romans watching Christians being devoured at the Coliseum."

"Really?" Elinor said. "How?"

"It just seems so brutal and senseless. What do they do with the bull afterward?" she asked Elinor, visibly in pain. She was very concerned. It was bothering her, like she was bothered by thinking about all the garbage.

"Well, I'm sure they don't recycle it, if that's what you mean?" Elinor suddenly said by accident. "I mean, they don't probably eat the meat. They do give the ear to the matador, if he is particularly good, or both if he is *really* good. And if he's *excellent*, they give him the tail."

Stephanie winced in pain. "I guess I didn't realize they still did such things. I suppose it's rather expensive, to go see, I mean."

"Yes, I think it is. Victor and I tried to get tickets once, but it was impossible. It's like the opera or theater. I think you have to book way in advance."

Stephanie tried to disguise her discomfort, horror really, at the idea that Elinor would want to see such a thing. It seemed that with every new bit Stephanie discovered of Europe, it gave her more evidence to prove her conviction that the people here had some clear flaw or kink in their humanity, that they were somehow fiercer than she. The subject was changed and Elinor asked her what her plans were for the summer. Were they escaping home as soon as school was out, Elinor supposed she wanted to know, or were they going to endure the summer here in France? "It really is perfect here. You can sleep with the windows open. It's so peaceful and quiet. It's never humid, and the flies and mosquitoes are very tame and well behaved, hardly noticeable at all," she said.

"Well, we really can't sleep with the windows open," Stephanie said, again as if even such a small pleasure was impossible for her to enjoy, considering her circumstances.

"Really? What do you mean?"

"Because it's too noisy in the city," she said. She went on to say that they had to endure the heat until August, because she didn't want to travel alone with the children and that Brad wouldn't take vacation until August when everything shut down for the summer holiday.

Elinor asked how he was doing now that his training was over.

"Well, he's just started his real job now, and he's the kind of person who really needs to be in full action, accomplishing things. He's out of town right now, and I suppose with his new job he'll have to travel quite a lot, too."

"Oh really?" Elinor said, perhaps with a note of concern. She wondered how Stephanie might manage that. Would the fact that he would be gone often make it any more difficult for her, she wondered. She seemed so apparently unhappy, and Elinor truly felt sorry for her. She seemed quite miserable. Perhaps she had a reason to be, she thought. It was not for her to determine what motivated her suffering.

"And how will you like that?" Elinor asked. "Do you think it will be very often?"

"Oh, fine," she said brightly in a way that at once threw off any concern she might have felt for her, smiling at Elinor.

"I suppose it is nice to be rid of one's husband from time to time," Elinor ventured.

"Yes," she agreed, "I certainly get more sleep when he's gone." They both smiled at each other.

"Husbands," Elinor said, "like death and taxes."

Stephanie smiled. "Hey, your sofa is great." She stood in the living room in contemplation, admiring the voluptuous curves of the Napolean III chartreuse sofa just recently delivered from the shop.

"It's so, well . . . frivolous," she said, her eyes following the curled sinews of the legs.

"I know. It's the color."

"Where did you find it?"

Elinor explained how she had been lured into the antique shop in town by a statue of John the Baptist in the window. He was rather rare and sought after and turned out to be far out of her price range, but when she turned to leave, she saw in the back the delightful chartreuse sofa.

"I couldn't believe it," she said. "It was just sitting there. The man kept trying to apologize for the upholstery, the color, I suppose, but it was the original upholstery and I would have to change it naturally, what would possibly go with that color. I agreed, nothing of course, and he gave it to me for four hundred dollars. Can you believe it? Victor's going to kill me. It is not like I need another sofa in the living room. We don't even really have room for it, but it was only four hundred dollars!"

"It's wonderful," she sighed. "Are you going to Deborah's wine tasting Saturday night?" Stephanie asked innocently.

"Deborah's having a wine tasting?"

Stephanie nodded slowly. "Sorry, I didn't know," she stopped.

Deborah was having a farewell gathering for Ruth Kimball, Stephanie told her, and to Elinor's surprise and, she admitted, indignation, she had been excluded. In fact, she had found herself to be increasingly excluded from things after apparently choosing to carry on a friendship with Béatrice, if one could call it that. It was becoming more and more remarked upon. The American women hated Béatrice, she could tell. They wanted an excuse to hate her, as Elinor was sure had happened to Béatrice before—perhaps throughout her life. Women always hate other women for being beautiful. If the French women could hate *them* for their ease with themselves and their spontaneity, it was only fair they should hate Béatrice for being beautiful, silent and bohemian. But perhaps it was more than that. Elinor's choosing Béatrice over them, the fact that Béatrice was French and that they should carry on in such an intimate manner was perhaps obscene and deserved to be punished with some clear message—that she would be rejected by all her friends for choosing to behave in such an unconventional manner. It became clear to Elinor that they, her other friends, wished to hate Béatrice, and she had given them a reason.

"A wine tasting?" Fabulous idea that Deborah had stolen from *her* as naturally as if it were a Bunko party and as neatly packaged with Phil and his friend Ted's expertise in wine, and she wasn't even invited!

Deborah congratulated herself on her superior taste and lovely children, but in fact the only thing she might for a moment hesitate on was her imagination. Apparently she was confident the community in general would agree with and support this sort of punishment for Elinor's unseemly behavior. Elinor supposed bitterly that Deborah thought the solution to her own dissatisfactions was in evening up the score, tit for tat. If Elinor was going to flaunt such a ready adaptability to the French language and culture, cultivating an appreciation for not only the food and wine, but for the women as well, stepping down off the curb away from her to accost that Frenchwoman in such an obvious way. Deborah would punish her for not following the rules while securing her own belief in them. Poor Deborah, Elinor thought, for missing the point entirely, and then she thought, no, too bad for me, for I shall be deserted by all my friends.

18

Deborah Knolls had her baby, and it was a beautiful baby boy.

"Hunter," she said proudly to the group that had gathered around the tiny thing, swaddled and bonneted in the car seat she held up for everyone's admiration.

"Hunter?" Elinor said confusedly. Hunter? Hunter Knolls? Oh my God! Deborah had named her baby a subdivision, she shrieked internally.

A shower had to be planned and a group gift thought of. Grace Elton placed herself in charge of organizing the event at her house—Grace knew that Deborah had talked of needing an Exersaucer, something Elinor had never heard of, but apparently it was a happier, healthier alternative to a baby walker which caused so much anxiety and certainly brain damage in the States and no properly concerned mother would think to use.

The scheme advanced, and Grace kept them abreast of her progress—an Exersaucer could not be found in all of Cherbourg! She had searched all of the possible baby depots and supermarkets, the Internet, perhaps one could be ordered from Toys R Us in Lyon, but then the French could never be expected to have such a thing anywhere, preferring either to inhibit their child's motor development or risk their tiny lives by putting them in the conventional walkers that could be found everywhere.

Some kind of alternative baby gym was found, and the final details of the shower were discussed outside the gate the afternoon before the shower. Deborah offered to bring her china because Grace seemed to be in a panic over not having enough coffee spoons, cups and saucers. The art of serving coffee in France required the proper dishes and utensils, for who had ever heard of a coffee spoon in the States or thought that it could be anything different than a teaspoon or that one couldn't simply swap one with the other.

"No, you'll upstage me," was Grace's answer. She was determined to pull the thing off herself and would not allow Deborah to take over and arrange her own shower. But Deborah fancied herself the expert in such affairs and could hardly resist helping to make it appropriately elegant. She secretly feared paper plates and plastic.

"Look Grace, we always share stuff like that, not everyone can be expected to have a set of Limoges china, and you haven't even been here a year. And besides, no one is trying to outdo each other *here*. Here in France, it's a bit like summer camp, you just don't know *who* you're going get thrown together with. But you end up being friends *anyway* and depending on one another." They all stood and stared at her. Suddenly Stephanie noticed Deborah had a little white spot on the shoulder of her lavender polo.

"Uh, Deborah," she said in a low voice, "I think you have bird poop on your shoulder."

Deborah was horrified and embarrassed.

"Oh *God*, you're kidding," she said in a panic, twisting her neck around and then trying frantically to brush it off with a tissue from her purse.

"Well, Deborah," Elinor said. "At least someone else isn't ashamed to sport pigeon poop on their shoulder."

Grace snorted, but the other ladies stood in a stunned silence.

Elinor shrugged, "Just another one of the hazards of living in France, I guess."

Deborah was beside herself, glaring at Elinor.

"Oh *God*, Elinor," she said with disgust, "get off your smug love affair with France—oh, the French? I think they're *charming*—and your open-ness and eagerness to embrace the culture *and* the people, I might add. Everyone's tired of it. Oh, don't get me wrong, I love the French, too, maybe just not in the same way *you* apparently do."

"What exactly do you mean, Deborah?" Elinor said.

"Oh, don't be so bourgeois, Elinor, as if you don't know exactly what I mean. You . . . and that *woman*. It's obvious you're in love with her."

Elinor thought she heard a gasp pass over the group like dominos col-lapsing in a wave, requiring seconds but seeming instantaneous.

"Yes, Deborah, I am," she said at last, "and let me compliment you on your perceptive curiosity in me. I believe you're right, I am in love with her in a way that is to you so incomprehensible, it would be ridiculous for me to explain it. But no, we are not lovers in the way that *you* would like to imagine," she heard herself say a bit breathless, looking around at the faces staring at her agape. "I simply have compassion for, okay, pas-sion for this woman. Deborah, you're so busy trying to be better than everyone else, you can never really *like* anyone. I just choose not to hold these people in contempt because they're different from me. It's their dif-ferences that have shown me myself and taught me to live," Elinor fin-ished and then stood feverishly for a moment and stared at the shocked faces of her friends, for at that moment some sweet new light glowed yellow upon the peeling whitewashed sides of the cement buildings of the bleak courtyard. She had deliberately emancipated herself from the restraints of society and convention and, of course, she knew she would never again be invited to anyone's dinners, so she turned and walked out of the courtyard into a blinding, new and mysterious world.

19

Deborah Knolls soon announced that she, too, was on her way home to the States at last. And what a happy future lay before her. Her successful husband had been given a handsome promotion, and there was little else to wish for in the way of achieving perfect happiness. She had just bought herself a new Louis Phillip buffet for her future dining room as a birthday present, "because when I asked Phil what he got me for my birthday, he said, 'I got you the United States of America for your birthday, what else do you need?'"

Grace Elton would stay. Her French had progressed to such a degree and her confidence increased to such a pitch that she didn't hesitate to accost Madame Lambert, the severe *directrice* of the school, with her frighteningly friendly and informal manner by insisting she *tutoyer* her and call her Grace, instead of insisting on such silly old-world formalities as using *madame*. She also eagerly announced that *SpongeBob SquarePants* had come to France and now French youngsters could enjoy watching *Bob L'Eponge* on Saturday mornings and be introduced to the kind of highbrow humor American kids have always taken for granted.

Elinor viewed her own departure with a mixture of sadness and relief. This adventure in France was so connected to Béatrice. Could she drop out of her own world, leave her family and live here forever? Like the hippie couple from Iowa she had met at the flea market on a Sunday who bought a house in the isolated village of Agiuperce—to choose to live among the retired village community who surely held them in contempt or at least at such a distance that they could only be considered a local curiosity. They were insane of course, maladapted to life in their own country, but then so had she become. But of course she could. There was so much to tempt her here, so much to interest her and occupy her when her life would normally be so ordinary in the States with all the unpleasantness of the climate and she would only be disappointed in everyone— the worst kind of snob.

Wasn't to live in France forever simply a matter of mastering the language? But it required much more than that—some great submission of her personality to have to adapt constantly in a culture that was not her own. It made her accept the loss of this beautiful place in exchange for knowing that she belonged and would be surrounded with people like herself, speak her mind easily and without effort. It was so important to her, she reluctantly accepted the loss of the sublime feeling of pleasure in her surroundings and Béatrice.

Elinor waited for Béatrice, quietly reading—trying to distract herself. *I am perfectly calm*, she said to herself although at the sound of any car's approach a flutter of her excitement licked at her belly like an unborn child. She sat in the house, quietly, safely, listening for Béatrice's car, hearing the engine strain and relax to help her park. She would simply plead that she must go, make Béatrice understand that they were insane to entertain such notions of love, and then she felt suddenly foolish because perhaps it was only she who entertained such notions. She heard a car door slam and Béatrice's footsteps on the pavement outside the house.

She went hastily into the kitchen and then when the doorbell rang, went to the door and swung it open. There was Béatrice, breathtakingly beautiful. Elinor suddenly hated her for it—for making her nervous like this.

"*Entrée,*" she said, leaning in for the customary air kisses, only they really kissed each other, Elinor placing her slightly parted lips on Béatrice's lovely cheek and kissing it deliberately. Although it was not yet noon, she was desperate to pour the wine. Thankfully, it was always acceptable in France.

"*Comment vas tu?*" she asked, trying to sound truly interested, feeling herself alert to the nearness of Béatrice, her scent, and the warmth of her body.

"*Pas tres bien.*"

Elinor went into the kitchen and poured them both a glass of wine. They sat on the chartreuse sofa. It was no larger than a love seat, and Elinor pushed herself up against the corner, giddy with Béatrice's nearness. She took a drink of her wine, nearly draining the glass. Although she had anticipated it since she had invited Béatrice, she now felt unequal to her heady presence in the house, alone. Elinor suddenly wanted to laugh out loud that she should feel so uneasy about having one of her women friends in the house alone. But the tension that existed between them seemed as furtive as any illicit rendezvous between a man and a woman. She tried to get past it, pretend as they were so skilled at pretending, that there was nothing at all suggestive in the way Béatrice leaned across her to get her purse from the table, reached in and took out a packet of photographs.

"These are the pictures from Paris," she said, leaning in closer and placing her other arm along the back of the sofa, Elinor noticed with some alarm. Béatrice moved in so close to her that Elinor could feel her breath and the heat of her body. Elinor admired the photos, looking at each one carefully, seeing Béatrice with her younger sister. Elinor was fascinated by what it must have been like to run around the city with her— quite like sisters themselves.

"*They're great,*" she said, feeling a little dizzy. She got up to go to the kitchen. Béatrice followed her. Elinor washed a bunch of grapes and set them in a bowl and offered them to Béatrice. Then she took out the ingredients for the salad she would make and set the frying pan on the stove, sprinkled it with olive oil and threw in *lardons* and pecans.

"It's nice to get away, although you always have to come back. Paris is nice, I feel I could disappear there," Béatrice hesitated, "or be anonymous. I don't know, perhaps it's a wish to be young again. It's filled with young people. I saw so many beautiful girls, models I suppose. I wondered what it must be like." She smiled at Elinor. It was a question, a suggestion.

Elinor stood near the stove, leaning on the sink, with her arms folded in front of her as if they could offer her some comfort or protection, and listened. She felt some eminent tragedy in what was happening. Béatrice seemed so sad. Elinor's departure was implied in everything she said, as if she must have Elinor understand her perfectly before it was too late. Or as if she, too, would have to leave. "Don't you ever want to escape?"

"Of course," Elinor said.

"But you're happy. You're happy with Victor? But don't tell me that you're perfectly satisfied either, you can't be. I look around and I wonder, I truly wonder, who is? I look at all the women at school and ask myself, can they actually enjoy this? I go to my cousin's wedding, and I think, why would you want to get married? What're you doing that for?"

Elinor laughed. She often thought the same thing.

"Tell me, what Victor's like. Is he interesting? Does he have right opinions?"

"Yes, he does," she said reluctantly. She didn't wish to boast of perfect happiness in the face of Béatrice's misery, but she had nothing to complain of and would be lying to claim dissatisfaction with a man who was entirely good. No, her desire for Béatrice had nothing to do with her dissatisfaction with Victor. Elinor turned her back to her and dumped the hot pecans and *lardons* into the salad and mixed the ingredients, concentrating on what she was doing, as if the task might calm her. Béatrice came up very close behind her and touched her lightly on the shoulder.

"Let me help you," she whispered. Elinor stood very still and quiet, frightened, because she suddenly knew Béatrice wanted to kiss her. She knew it as clearly as if it had been spoken or asked—as clearly as she knew a boy in college wanted to kiss her in the kitchen at a party. She lost her nerve and recommenced tossing the salad.

"Let me just add the dressing," she managed, and then turned to Béatrice with the bowl in front of her. They met each other's gaze, and Elinor smiled apologetically. She handed the salad to Béatrice and took the wine to the table, and they both sat down to eat.

"Je n'ai plus envie de coucher avec lui. I don't want to sleep with him anymore," Béatrice said.

"Who does? Nobody actually wants to sleep with their own husband," Elinor said, pretending they were just having girl talk, the kind that is so common among girlfriends. Talk that she often had with the ladies at coffee. But Elinor knew what Béatrice meant. She was begging her for something, and this plea had hung between them almost from their first acquaintance, although it was never articulated. Elinor played the part of sympathetic friend as they both expected her to and said she understood what she meant, that this kind of indifference was natural and inevitable. She took a long drink of her wine and refilled the glass. The denial was brutal.

"Il n'est pas gentil. But perhaps I'm not either," Béatrice said.

"Mais, non. What do you mean, of course you are."

"No, I really don't think I am. I'm miserable, *Alienor,"* she said meaningfully, and Elinor was charmed with the French pronunciation of her name. "I don't love him anymore, we don't make each other happy. I want . . . I want to escape. Men are so tiresome. It is impossible to be with him. We're too different. We say so little to one another."

As typical as her complaint was, Elinor was beside herself. She felt suddenly unsteady as if she would faint and couldn't exactly focus on what she was saying. Certainly he had loved her selfishly because she was beautiful, and he had wanted her all to himself so that his possessiveness, her babies, his children had reduced her to something he could now feel nothing but contempt for. Is he so stupid and selfish? What? Does he fancy himself Lawrence of Arabia, going off to save subjugated cultures, in love with adventure, but incapable of loving his wife? Elinor wanted to know. Was he gay? He certainly was handsome and elegant, and he certainly had an air of being unfaithful.

"What?" Elinor asked, "what is it? Does he cheat on you?" she finally asked, but at the same time, she didn't want to know the ugly truth of this cliché—that Béatrice still had to sleep with him even though he fucked other women. She was too exhausted. What could be more useless than a husband without work who sleeps around? It was brutal to be insincere, to keep her true feelings under such tight regulation, and she knocked back another glass of wine. So desperately did she want to escape her longing, she was willing to hate Béatrice or at least be disgusted with her.

"Everyone wants to get married and live happily ever after. Everyone thinks, hopes, they will. The dull reality is it's not possible, and it becomes a long haul. I'm sure it's my fault," she said.

Elinor was prepared to be bored with the wayward French husband. It seemed at once hilarious and tragic, but Elinor did not despise her for it when Béatrice was the closest thing to herself she had ever understood as plainly, openly, and honestly as her own husband and daughters, and she knew that she was both saved and lost with her.

"Have you never thought of what it would be like with a girl?" Béatrice asked. Their eyes met in understanding. Béatrice had spoken it, asked the question that was every day implied but never expressed. She reached around to take the fastener from her hair and shake it out to run her fingers through it, in exhaustion and frustration. It was as flirtatious a gesture as any high school girl might employ. Her hair fell around her face, and Elinor was surprised to see that she had cut it and, now, it hung just below her jaw. Béatrice had cut her long brunette hair into a kind of bob with a thick wavy tress that fell before her face. Elinor was breathless, the effect was so charming and lovely. She leaned toward her to reach out and touch it absently with her fingers, emboldened by the wine. "Yes," she whispered, "ever since I met you. It's lovely," she said matter-of-factly, looking at her beautiful friend. The ingenuousness of the compliment calmed her, and she slid her fingers to the back of Béatrice's neck. She had a great desire to comfort her and was terrified of disappointing her.

"Je te connais, Béatrice. Je te connais," she breathed.

Elinor knew now as she had not allowed herself to know before that she wanted Béatrice in the same way a man wants a woman. Wanted to possess her in the only way possible to end the agony of her attraction and that was to hold her, know every part of her body as only a lover could. It seemed natural for two married women so practiced in the routine of sex with their husbands to desire each other in this new and fascinating way. And Elinor pulled her toward her. With a purpose that surprised her, Elinor brought her mouth down on hers so that she felt Béatrice's teeth against her lips, and she wished to hurt her as she felt she had been hurt, tortured by what she felt for so long. Fear and desire throbbed in her head, and she felt hot and drunk with the headiness of the wine. She felt Béatrice's mouth open slightly to receive the kiss and kiss her back with an urgency that confirmed there was very little time. But it was more than that—their lives seemed to be running out like sand through their fingers while they handed themselves out to everyone—husbands and children.

All the women on the courtyard of the school yard that day would know nothing of what it was to love each other and they both stood, trembling, reaching for each other. Here was Béatrice, beautiful, French, kissing her with the same curiosity she might devote to a television documentary on mushrooms or fish—tasting Elinor's mouth as if it were a fine imported wine. Elinor felt suddenly hot and foolish—a blush rushing over the surface of her skin with some astonishing significance that she should be forever stained by. She pulled away.

"Forgive me, Béatrice. You're so lovely," she said, closing her mouth into a smile, as if she were thanking her for some thoughtful favor or concern. Béatrice reached out and caressed her cheek lightly. Her calm smile reassured Elinor everything was as natural as the gathering of clouds before a storm that raged against the earth, only to bring calm cool breezes that cleared away the darkness with the warmth of the sun, kissing and blessing the earth again so that the children could be let out to run and play. Until now, Elinor's sole way of keeping the devil in the garden at bay was to decide to do nothing. Do absolutely nothing, and it was so unbearable that she might have wished she was dead. But now she had done something, acted, and she was both miserable and ecstatic, liberated and ensnared. Béatrice was not likely to sacrifice her own pleasure for any moral conflict or puritan remorse, and Elinor was at once envious of her incredible calm. Béatrice's life would be filled with much the same drama and chaos and profound feelings of failure as any woman feels in the silence of an empty house, and Elinor would share these feelings with her quietly, inside her head for the rest of her life and think to herself, *I wonder. I wonder if she feels the same way.*

"I will never forget you." Elinor said and did what seemed so impossible to do—she said good-bye.

"Au revoir," she said and watched Béatrice turn and go. As much as she wished to, she did not call her back or go after her, or try to hold on to her, knowing that the memory of her would be her silent companion, keep her company in her lonely days that would certainly be a part of her life ahead. But maybe, she hoped, maybe when they had grown old and their children were raised and their husbands tired of them, Elinor would meet her in Paris, she thought, and held on to this wish as she left the house to pick up the children.

Elinor walked onto the school yard alone and searched the lovely heads of the children for Alexi. She found her near the wall, whispering, telling a secret to a dark headed French girl on the playground. They both giggled and then ran off together hand in hand after the others, and Elinor watched fascinated and slightly envious because suddenly she knew her daughter would grow up beautiful and fall in love someday, and she hoped that it would be as exquisite, new, and intense as childhood itself. She walked up to Alexi and took her small hand in hers and said, "Alexi, say good-bye, it's time to go."

About the Author

The author graduated from the University of Illinois and holds a master's degree in English from Converse College. She lives and writes in France and the United States.

Visit

Spinsters Ink

at

spinstersink.com

or call our toll-free number

1-800-301-6860

Publications from Spinsters Ink

P.O. Box 242
Midway, Florida 32343
Phone: 800 301-6860
www.spinstersink.com

DISORDERLY ATTACHMENT by Jennifer L. Jordan. 5th Kristin Ashe Mystery. Kris investigates whether a mansion someone wants to convert into condos is haunted.   ISBN 1-883523-74-5 $14.95

VERA'S STILL POINT by Ruth Perkinson. Vera is reminded of exactly what it is that she has been missing in life.
                                      ISBN 1-883523-73-7 $14.95

OUTRAGEOUS by Sheila-Ortiz Taylor. Arden Benbow, a motorcycle riding, lesbian Latina poet from LA is hired to teach poetry in a small liberal arts college in northwest Florida.
                                      ISBN 1-883523-72-9 $14.95

UNBREAKABLE by Blayne Cooper. The bonds of love and friendship can be as strong as steel. But are they unbreakable?
                                      ISBN 1-883523-76-1 $14.95

ALL BETS OFF by Jaime Clevenger. Bette Lawrence is about to find out how hard life can be for someone of low society standing in the 1900s.   ISBN 1-883523-71-0 $14.95

UNBEARABLE LOSSES by Jennifer L. Jordan. 4th in the Kristin Ashe Mystery series. Two elderly sisters have hired Kris to discover who is pilfering from their award-winning holiday display.
                                      ISBN 1-883523-68-0 $14.95

FRENCH POSTCARDS by Jane Merchant. When Elinor moves to France with her husband and two children, she never expects that her life is about to be changed forever.   ISBN 1-883523-67-2 $14.95

EXISTING SOLUTIONS by Jennifer L. Jordan. 2nd book in the Kristin Ashe Mystery series. When Kris is hired to find an activist's biological father, things get complicated when she finds herself falling for her client.   ISBN 1-883523-69-9 $14.95

A SAFE PLACE TO SLEEP by Jennifer L. Jordan. 1st in the Kristin Ashe Mystery series. Kris is approached by well known lesbian Destiny Greaves with an unusual request. One that will lead Kris to hunt for her own missing childhood pieces.   ISBN 1-883523-70-2 $14.95